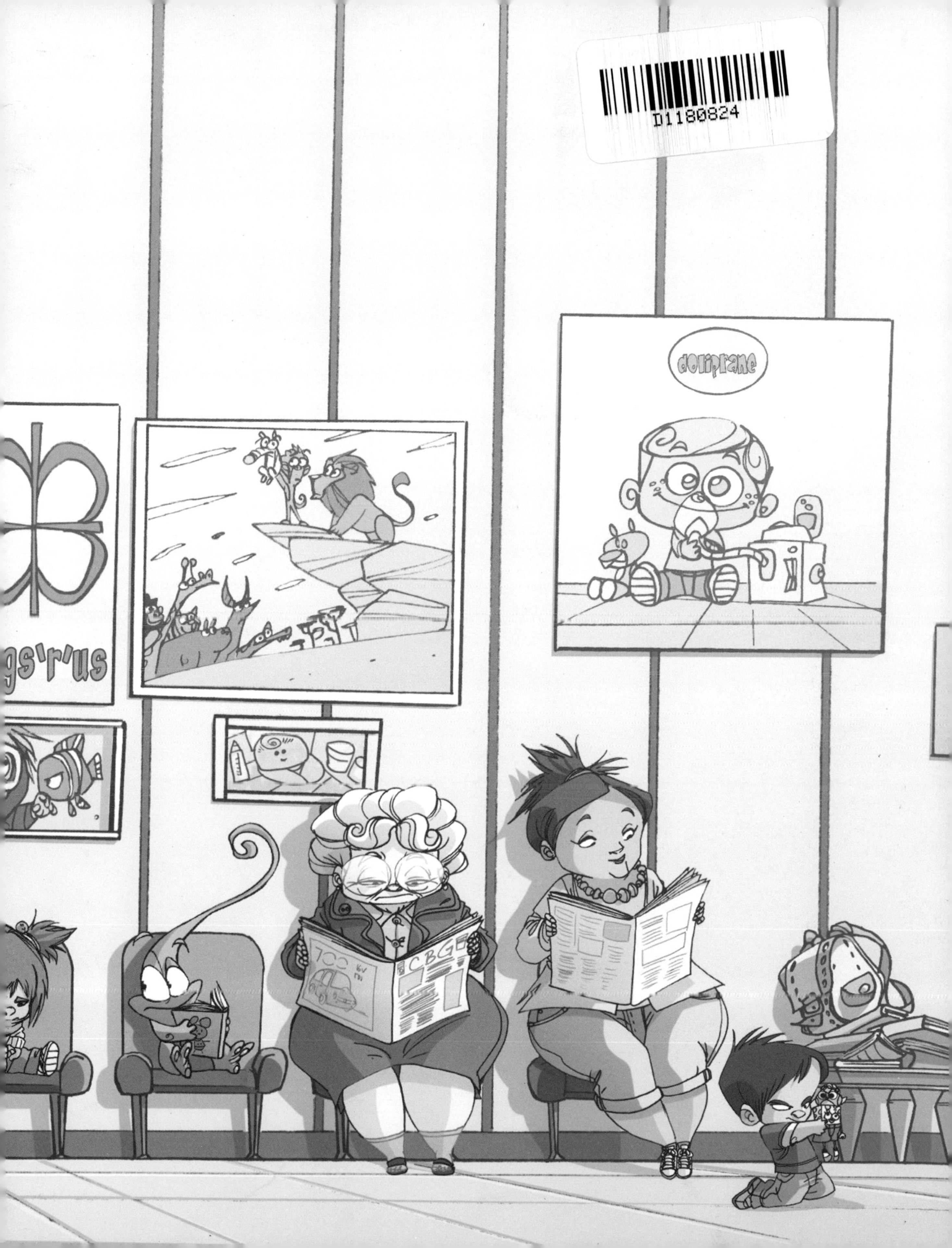
doliprane
gs'r'us
CBG

Ernest&Rebecca

2

"Sam the Repulsive"

Guillaume Bianco — Writer
Antonello Dalena — Artist
Cecilia Giumento — Colorist

PAPERCUTZ™
New York

Mommy

She's the most beautiful mommy of all! She's not at home a lot because of her job, but she always finds time to cook my favorite food for me: "steak and fries with ketchup and mayonnaise!"

Daddy

He's an artist. A painter... like Picasso, but better! We have lots of fun together when mommy's at work... He's the funniest daddy of all!

Coralie

She's my big sister. I adore her, even if, ever since she's been in her rebellious stage, she stays in her room all the time.

Dr. Fakbert

He's awful as a doctor. He often comes to the house to take care of me... You've got to wonder why I'm always sick!

Ernest

He's a microbe... and he's my best friend! I caught him one day while on a frog hunt. Since then, we're always together... He's super smart and really strong: he can change into anything!

And me: Rebecca!

I'm not very big... It's 'cause I hate soup! I'd rather eat ketchup and chase frogs with Ernest in the rain!

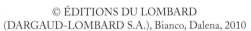

Ernest & Rebecca
#2 "Sam the Repulsive"

Guillaume Bianco – Writer
Antonello Dalena – Artist
Cecilia Giumento – Colorist
Jean-Luc Deglin – Original Design
Joe Johnson – Translation
Janice Chiang – Lettering
Production – Nelson Design Group, LLC
Associate Editor – Michael Petranek
Jim Salicrup
Editor-in-Chief

© ÉDITIONS DU LOMBARD
(DARGAUD-LOMBARD S.A.), Bianco, Dalena, 2010
www.lombard.com
All rights reserved.
English Translation and other editorial matter
Copyright © 2012 by Papercutz.
ISBN: 978-1-59707-299-1

Printed in China
February 2012 by New Era Printing LTD.
Trend Centre, 29-31 Cheung Lee St.
Rm. 1101-1103, 11F, Chaiwan, Hong Kong

Distributed by Macmillan.
First Papercutz Printing

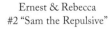

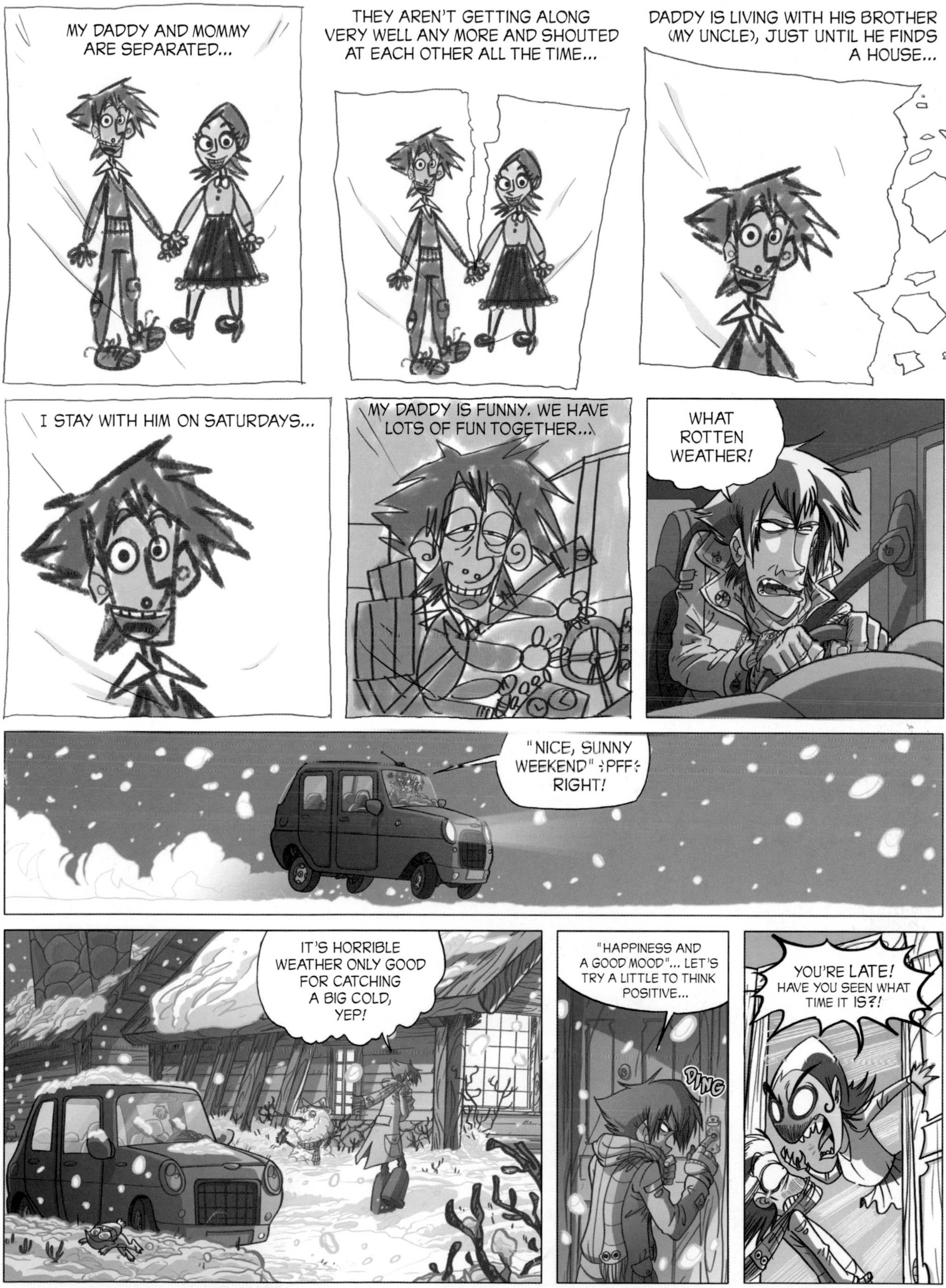

MY DADDY AND MOMMY ARE SEPARATED...
THEY AREN'T GETTING ALONG VERY WELL ANY MORE AND SHOUTED AT EACH OTHER ALL THE TIME...
DADDY IS LIVING WITH HIS BROTHER (MY UNCLE), JUST UNTIL HE FINDS A HOUSE...
I STAY WITH HIM ON SATURDAYS...
MY DADDY IS FUNNY. WE HAVE LOTS OF FUN TOGETHER...
WHAT ROTTEN WEATHER!
"NICE, SUNNY WEEKEND" ÷PFF÷ RIGHT!
IT'S HORRIBLE WEATHER ONLY GOOD FOR CATCHING A BIG COLD, YEP!
"HAPPINESS AND A GOOD MOOD"... LET'S TRY A LITTLE TO THINK POSITIVE...
DING
YOU'RE LATE! HAVE YOU SEEN WHAT TIME IT IS?!

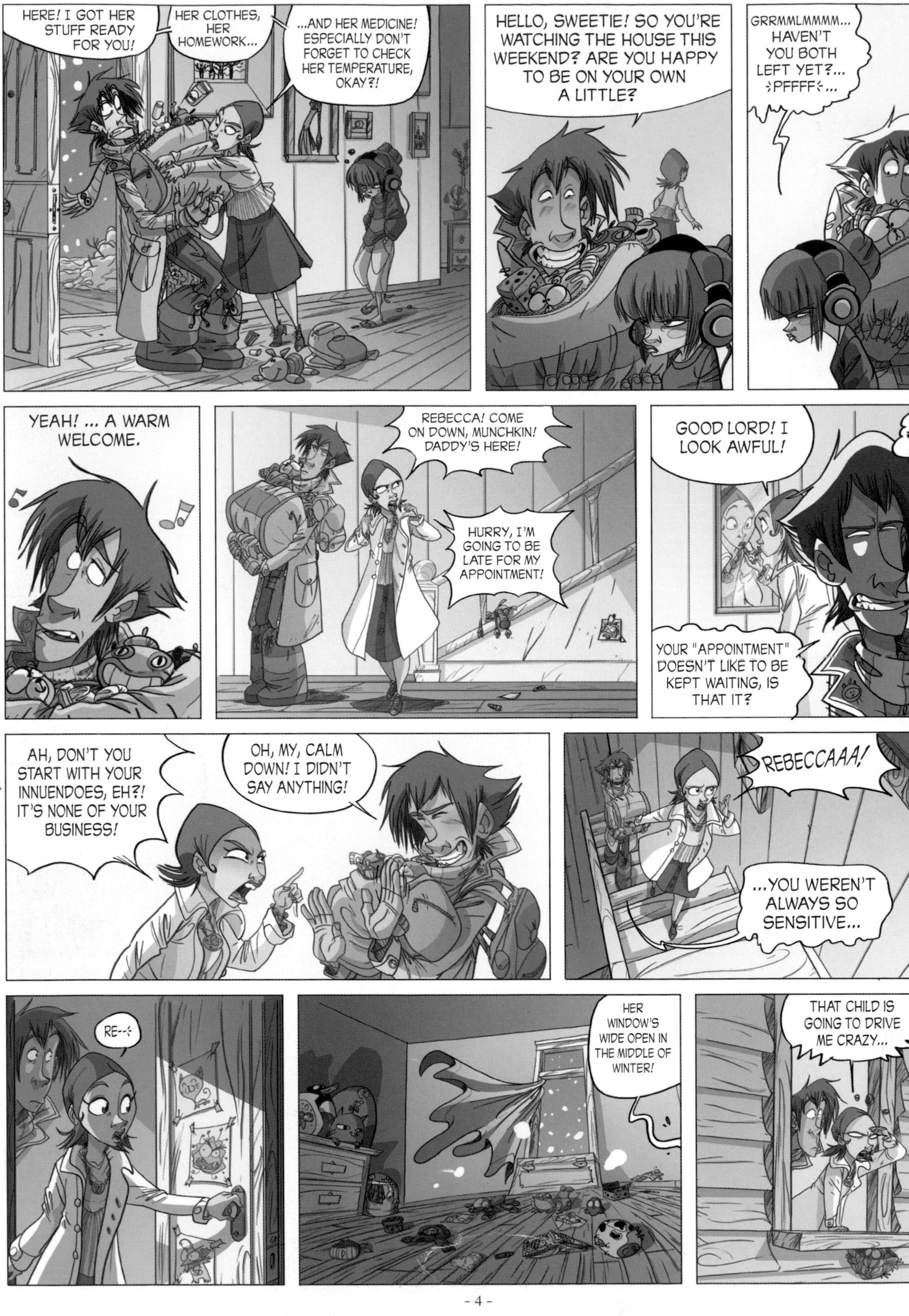
HERE! I GOT HER STUFF READY FOR YOU!
HER CLOTHES, HER HOMEWORK...
...AND HER MEDICINE! ESPECIALLY DON'T FORGET TO CHECK HER TEMPERATURE, OKAY?!
HELLO, SWEETIE! SO YOU'RE WATCHING THE HOUSE THIS WEEKEND? ARE YOU HAPPY TO BE ON YOUR OWN A LITTLE?
GRRMMLMMMM... HAVEN'T YOU BOTH LEFT YET?... PFFFF...
YEAH! ... A WARM WELCOME.
REBECCA! COME ON DOWN, MUNCHKIN! DADDY'S HERE!
HURRY, I'M GOING TO BE LATE FOR MY APPOINTMENT!
GOOD LORD! I LOOK AWFUL!
YOUR "APPOINTMENT" DOESN'T LIKE TO BE KEPT WAITING, IS THAT IT?
AH, DON'T YOU START WITH YOUR INNUENDOES, EH?! IT'S NONE OF YOUR BUSINESS!
OH, MY, CALM DOWN! I DIDN'T SAY ANYTHING!
REBECCAAA!
...YOU WEREN'T ALWAYS SO SENSITIVE...
RE--
HER WINDOW'S WIDE OPEN IN THE MIDDLE OF WINTER!
THAT CHILD IS GOING TO DRIVE ME CRAZY...

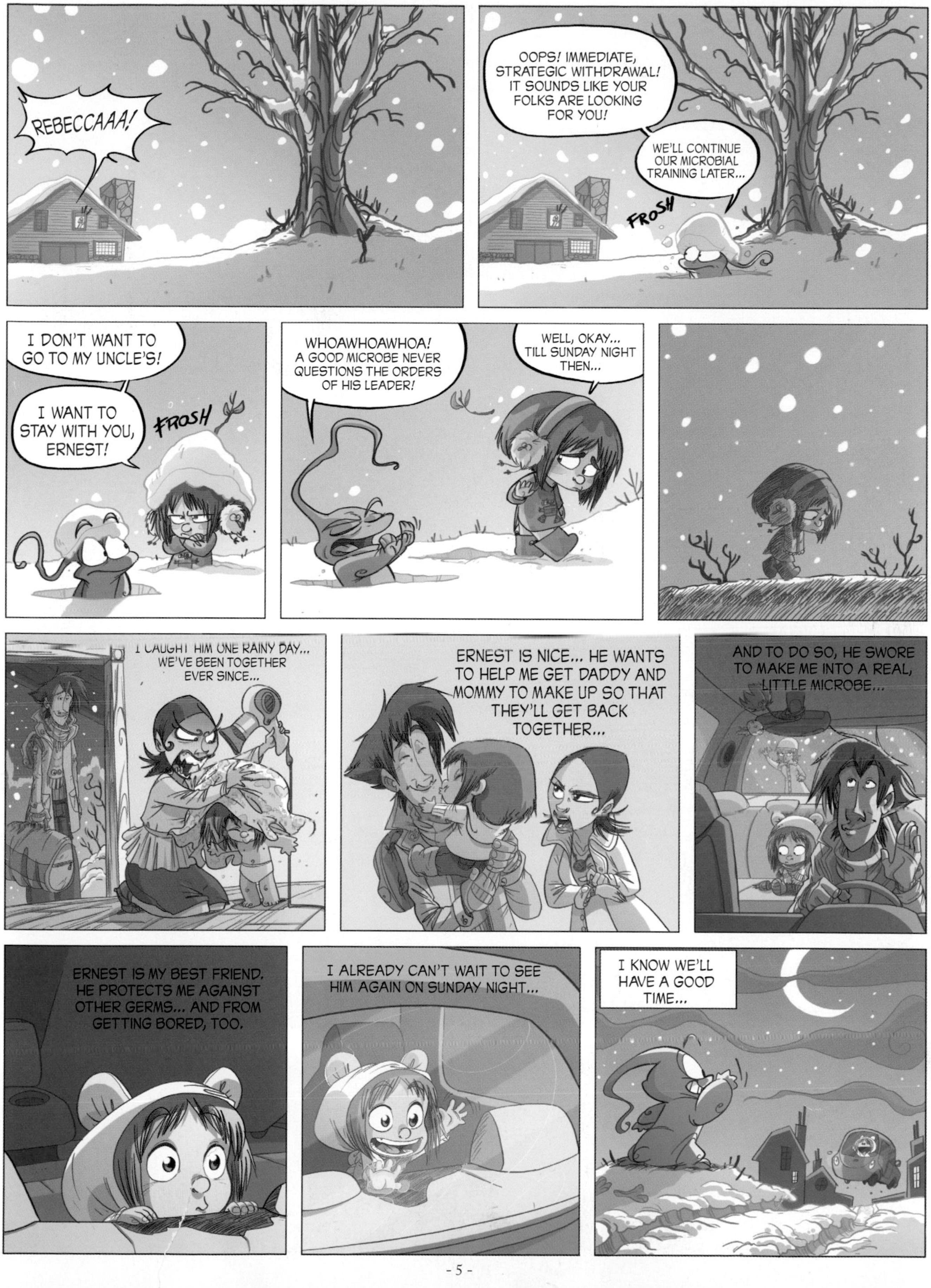
REBECCAAA!
OOPS! IMMEDIATE, STRATEGIC WITHDRAWAL! IT SOUNDS LIKE YOUR FOLKS ARE LOOKING FOR YOU!
WE'LL CONTINUE OUR MICROBIAL TRAINING LATER...
FROSH
I DON'T WANT TO GO TO MY UNCLE'S!
I WANT TO STAY WITH YOU, ERNEST!
FROSH
WHOAWHOAWHOA! A GOOD MICROBE NEVER QUESTIONS THE ORDERS OF HIS LEADER!
WELL, OKAY... TILL SUNDAY NIGHT THEN...
I CAUGHT HIM ONE RAINY DAY... WE'VE BEEN TOGETHER EVER SINCE...
ERNEST IS NICE... HE WANTS TO HELP ME GET DADDY AND MOMMY TO MAKE UP SO THAT THEY'LL GET BACK TOGETHER...
AND TO DO SO, HE SWORE TO MAKE ME INTO A REAL, LITTLE MICROBE...
ERNEST IS MY BEST FRIEND. HE PROTECTS ME AGAINST OTHER GERMS... AND FROM GETTING BORED, TOO.
I ALREADY CAN'T WAIT TO SEE HIM AGAIN ON SUNDAY NIGHT...
I KNOW WE'LL HAVE A GOOD TIME...

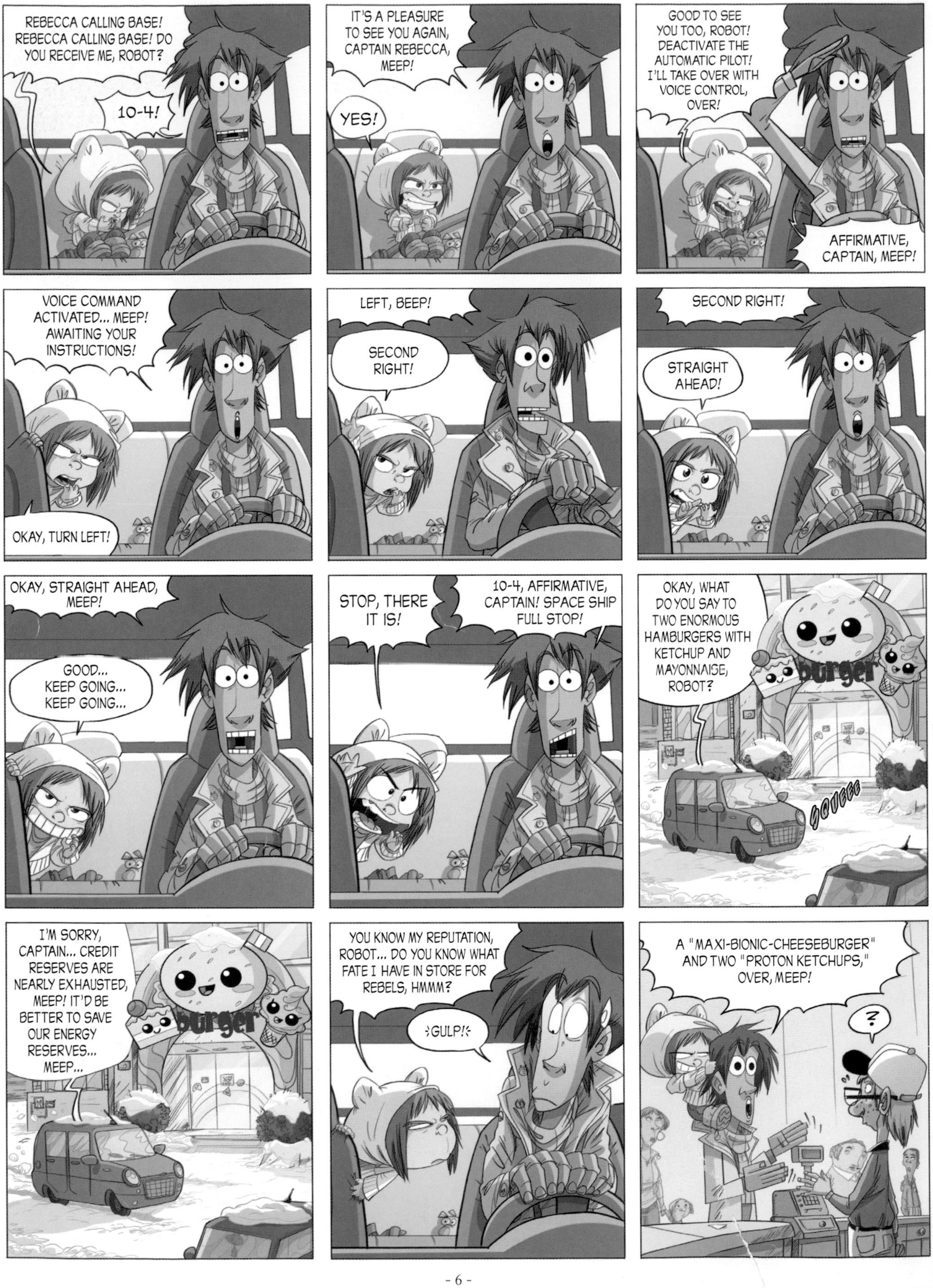

REBECCA CALLING BASE! REBECCA CALLING BASE! DO YOU RECEIVE ME, ROBOT?
10-4!
IT'S A PLEASURE TO SEE YOU AGAIN, CAPTAIN REBECCA, MEEP!
YES!
GOOD TO SEE YOU TOO, ROBOT! DEACTIVATE THE AUTOMATIC PILOT! I'LL TAKE OVER WITH VOICE CONTROL, OVER!
AFFIRMATIVE, CAPTAIN, MEEP!
VOICE COMMAND ACTIVATED... MEEP! AWAITING YOUR INSTRUCTIONS!
OKAY, TURN LEFT!
LEFT, BEEP!
SECOND RIGHT!
SECOND RIGHT!
STRAIGHT AHEAD!
OKAY, STRAIGHT AHEAD, MEEP!
GOOD... KEEP GOING... KEEP GOING...
STOP, THERE IT IS!
10-4, AFFIRMATIVE, CAPTAIN! SPACE SHIP FULL STOP!
OKAY, WHAT DO YOU SAY TO TWO ENORMOUS HAMBURGERS WITH KETCHUP AND MAYONNAISE, ROBOT?
burger
SQUEEE
I'M SORRY, CAPTAIN... CREDIT RESERVES ARE NEARLY EXHAUSTED, MEEP! IT'D BE BETTER TO SAVE OUR ENERGY RESERVES... MEEP...
burger
YOU KNOW MY REPUTATION, ROBOT... DO YOU KNOW WHAT FATE I HAVE IN STORE FOR REBELS, HMMM?
GULP!
A "MAXI-BIONIC-CHEESEBURGER" AND TWO "PROTON KETCHUPS," OVER, MEEP!
?

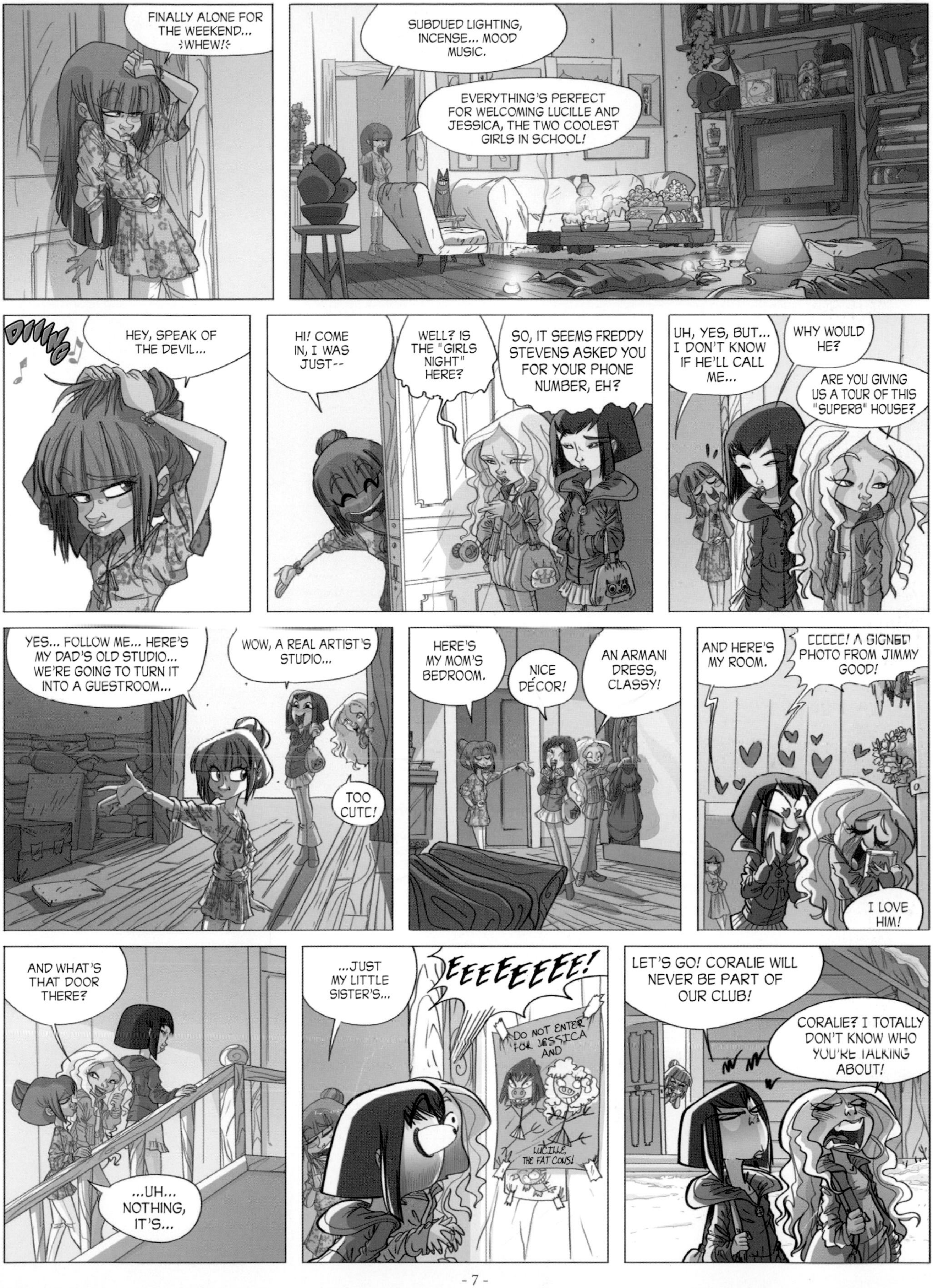
FINALLY ALONE FOR THE WEEKEND... WHEW!
SUBDUED LIGHTING, INCENSE... MOOD MUSIC.
EVERYTHING'S PERFECT FOR WELCOMING LUCILLE AND JESSICA, THE TWO COOLEST GIRLS IN SCHOOL!
DIIING
HEY, SPEAK OF THE DEVIL...
HI! COME IN, I WAS JUST--
WELL? IS THE "GIRLS NIGHT" HERE?
SO, IT SEEMS FREDDY STEVENS ASKED YOU FOR YOUR PHONE NUMBER, EH?
UH, YES, BUT... I DON'T KNOW IF HE'LL CALL ME...
WHY WOULD HE?
ARE YOU GIVING US A TOUR OF THIS "SUPERB" HOUSE?
YES... FOLLOW ME... HERE'S MY DAD'S OLD STUDIO... WE'RE GOING TO TURN IT INTO A GUESTROOM...
WOW, A REAL ARTIST'S STUDIO...
TOO CUTE!
HERE'S MY MOM'S BEDROOM.
NICE DÉCOR!
AN ARMANI DRESS, CLASSY!
AND HERE'S MY ROOM.
EEEEE! A SIGNED PHOTO FROM JIMMY GOOD!
I LOVE HIM!
AND WHAT'S THAT DOOR THERE?
...UH... NOTHING, IT'S...
...JUST MY LITTLE SISTER'S...
EEEEEEEE!
DO NOT ENTER FOR JESSICA AND LUCILLE, THE FAT COWS!
LET'S GO! CORALIE WILL NEVER BE PART OF OUR CLUB!
CORALIE? I TOTALLY DON'T KNOW WHO YOU'RE TALKING ABOUT!

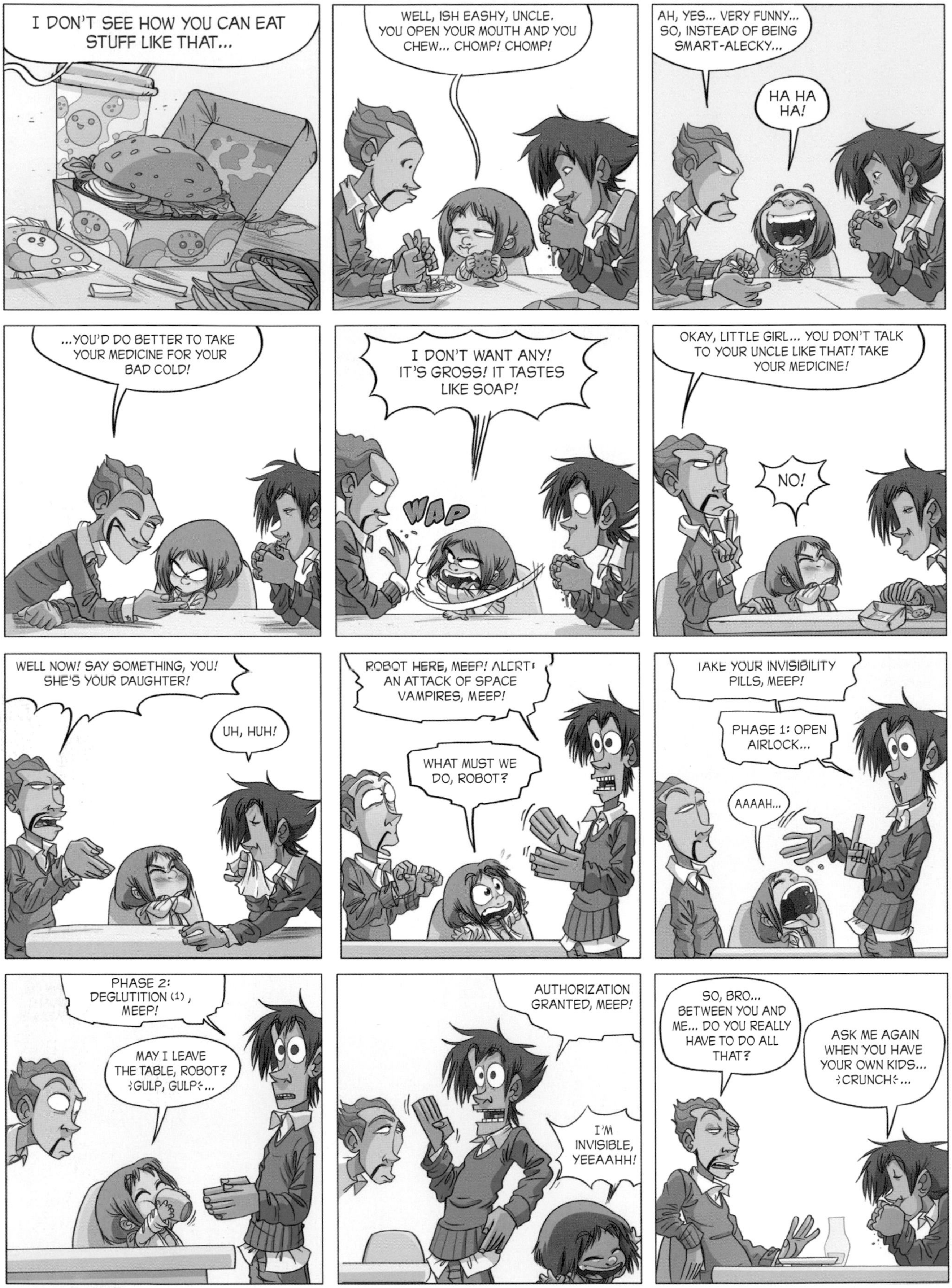
I DON'T SEE HOW YOU CAN EAT STUFF LIKE THAT...
WELL, ISH EASHY, UNCLE. YOU OPEN YOUR MOUTH AND YOU CHEW... CHOMP! CHOMP!
AH, YES... VERY FUNNY... SO, INSTEAD OF BEING SMART-ALECKY...
HA HA HA!
...YOU'D DO BETTER TO TAKE YOUR MEDICINE FOR YOUR BAD COLD!
I DON'T WANT ANY! IT'S GROSS! IT TASTES LIKE SOAP!
WAP
OKAY, LITTLE GIRL... YOU DON'T TALK TO YOUR UNCLE LIKE THAT! TAKE YOUR MEDICINE!
NO!
WELL NOW! SAY SOMETHING, YOU! SHE'S YOUR DAUGHTER!
UH, HUH!
ROBOT HERE, MEEP! ALERT! AN ATTACK OF SPACE VAMPIRES, MEEP!
WHAT MUST WE DO, ROBOT?
TAKE YOUR INVISIBILITY PILLS, MEEP!
PHASE 1: OPEN AIRLOCK...
AAAAH...
PHASE 2: DEGLUTITION (1), MEEP!
MAY I LEAVE THE TABLE, ROBOT? ⊰GULP, GULP⊱...
AUTHORIZATION GRANTED, MEEP!
I'M INVISIBLE, YEEAAHH!
SO, BRO... BETWEEN YOU AND ME... DO YOU REALLY HAVE TO DO ALL THAT?
ASK ME AGAIN WHEN YOU HAVE YOUR OWN KIDS... ⊰CRUNCH⊱...

(1) THE PROCESS OF SWALLOWING.

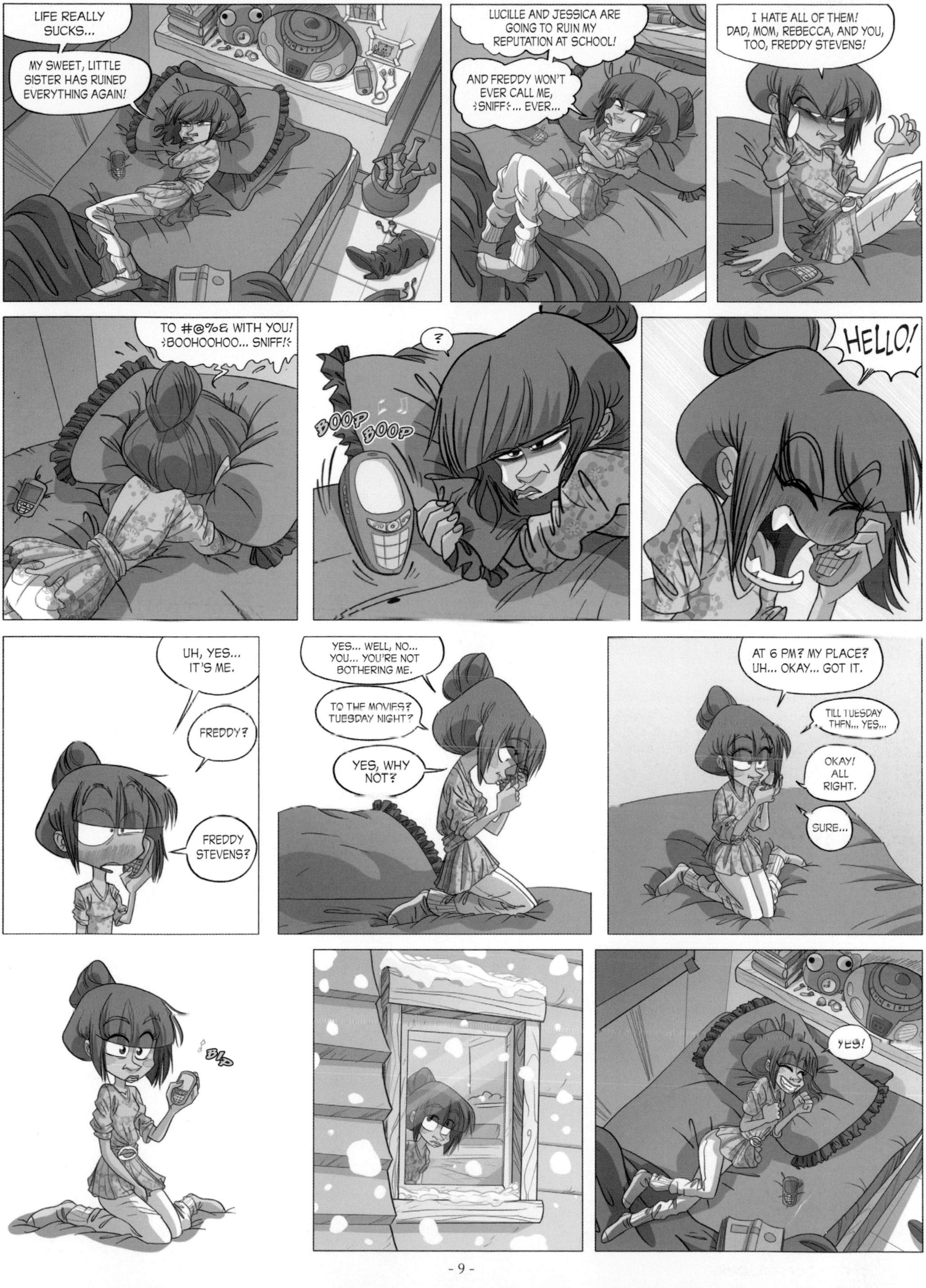

LIFE REALLY SUCKS...
MY SWEET, LITTLE SISTER HAS RUINED EVERYTHING AGAIN!
LUCILLE AND JESSICA ARE GOING TO RUIN MY REPUTATION AT SCHOOL!
AND FREDDY WON'T EVER CALL ME, ⸗SNIFF⸗... EVER...
I HATE ALL OF THEM! DAD, MOM, REBECCA, AND YOU, TOO, FREDDY STEVENS!
TO #@%& WITH YOU! ⸗BOOHOOHOO... SNIFF!⸗
?
BOOP BOOP
HELLO!
UH, YES... IT'S ME.
FREDDY?
FREDDY STEVENS?
YES... WELL, NO... YOU... YOU'RE NOT BOTHERING ME.
TO THE MOVIES? TUESDAY NIGHT?
YES, WHY NOT?
AT 6 PM? MY PLACE? UH... OKAY... GOT IT.
TILL TUESDAY THEN... YES...
OKAY! ALL RIGHT.
SURE...
BIP
YES!

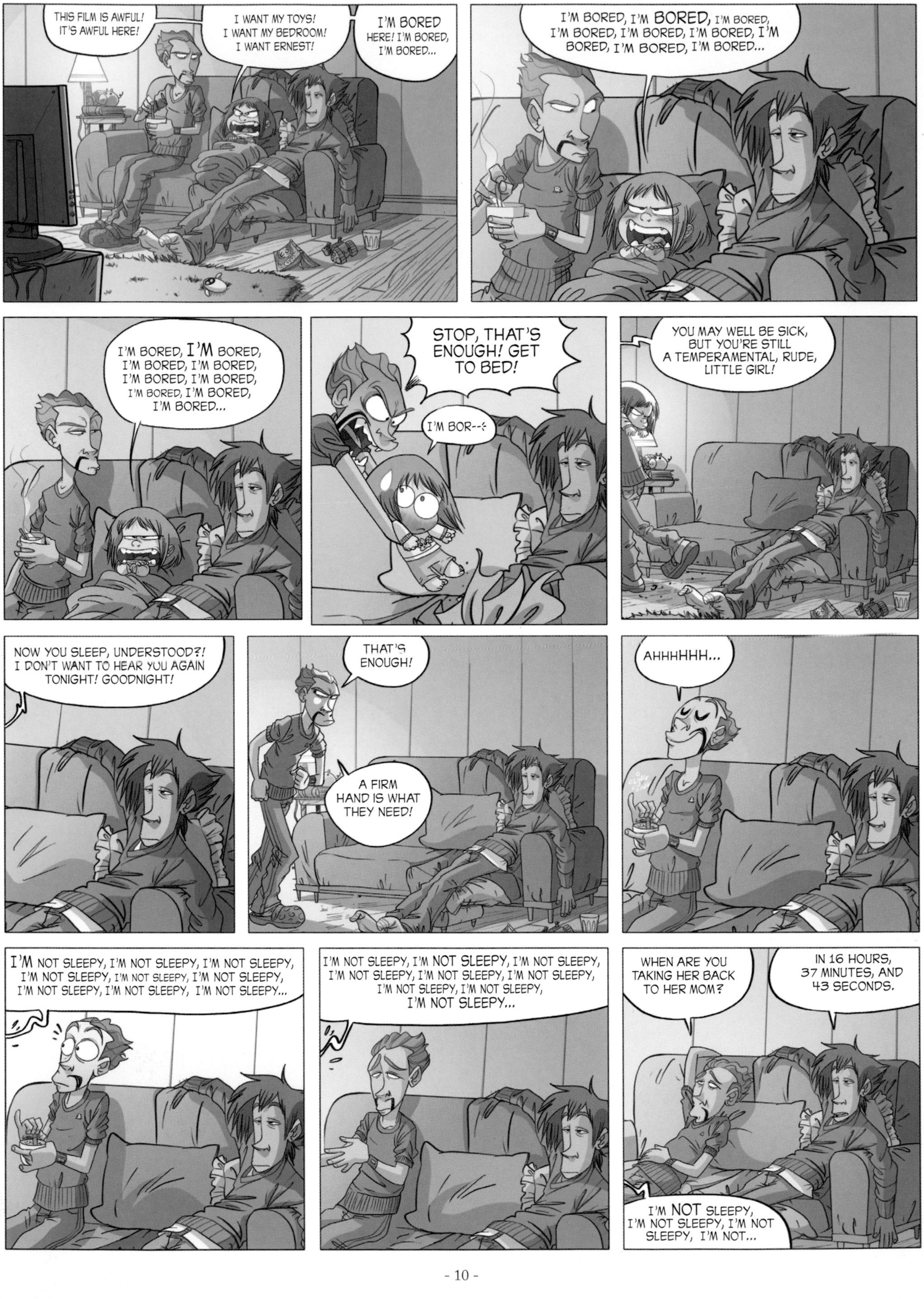
THIS FILM IS AWFUL! IT'S AWFUL HERE!
I WANT MY TOYS! I WANT MY BEDROOM! I WANT ERNEST!
I'M BORED HERE! I'M BORED, I'M BORED...
I'M BORED, I'M BORED, I'M BORED, I'M BORED, I'M BORED, I'M BORED, I'M BORED, I'M BORED, I'M BORED, I'M BORED...
I'M BORED, I'M BORED, I'M BORED, I'M BORED, I'M BORED, I'M BORED, I'M BORED, I'M BORED, I'M BORED...
STOP, THAT'S ENOUGH! GET TO BED!
I'M BOR--
YOU MAY WELL BE SICK, BUT YOU'RE STILL A TEMPERAMENTAL, RUDE, LITTLE GIRL!
NOW YOU SLEEP, UNDERSTOOD?! I DON'T WANT TO HEAR YOU AGAIN TONIGHT! GOODNIGHT!
THAT'S ENOUGH!
A FIRM HAND IS WHAT THEY NEED!
AHHHHHH...
I'M NOT SLEEPY, I'M NOT SLEEPY, I'M NOT SLEEPY, I'M NOT SLEEPY, I'M NOT SLEEPY, I'M NOT SLEEPY, I'M NOT SLEEPY, I'M NOT SLEEPY, I'M NOT SLEEPY...
I'M NOT SLEEPY, I'M NOT SLEEPY, I'M NOT SLEEPY, I'M NOT SLEEPY, I'M NOT SLEEPY, I'M NOT SLEEPY, I'M NOT SLEEPY, I'M NOT SLEEPY, I'M NOT SLEEPY...
WHEN ARE YOU TAKING HER BACK TO HER MOM?
IN 16 HOURS, 37 MINUTES, AND 43 SECONDS.
I'M NOT SLEEPY, I'M NOT SLEEPY, I'M NOT SLEEPY, I'M NOT...

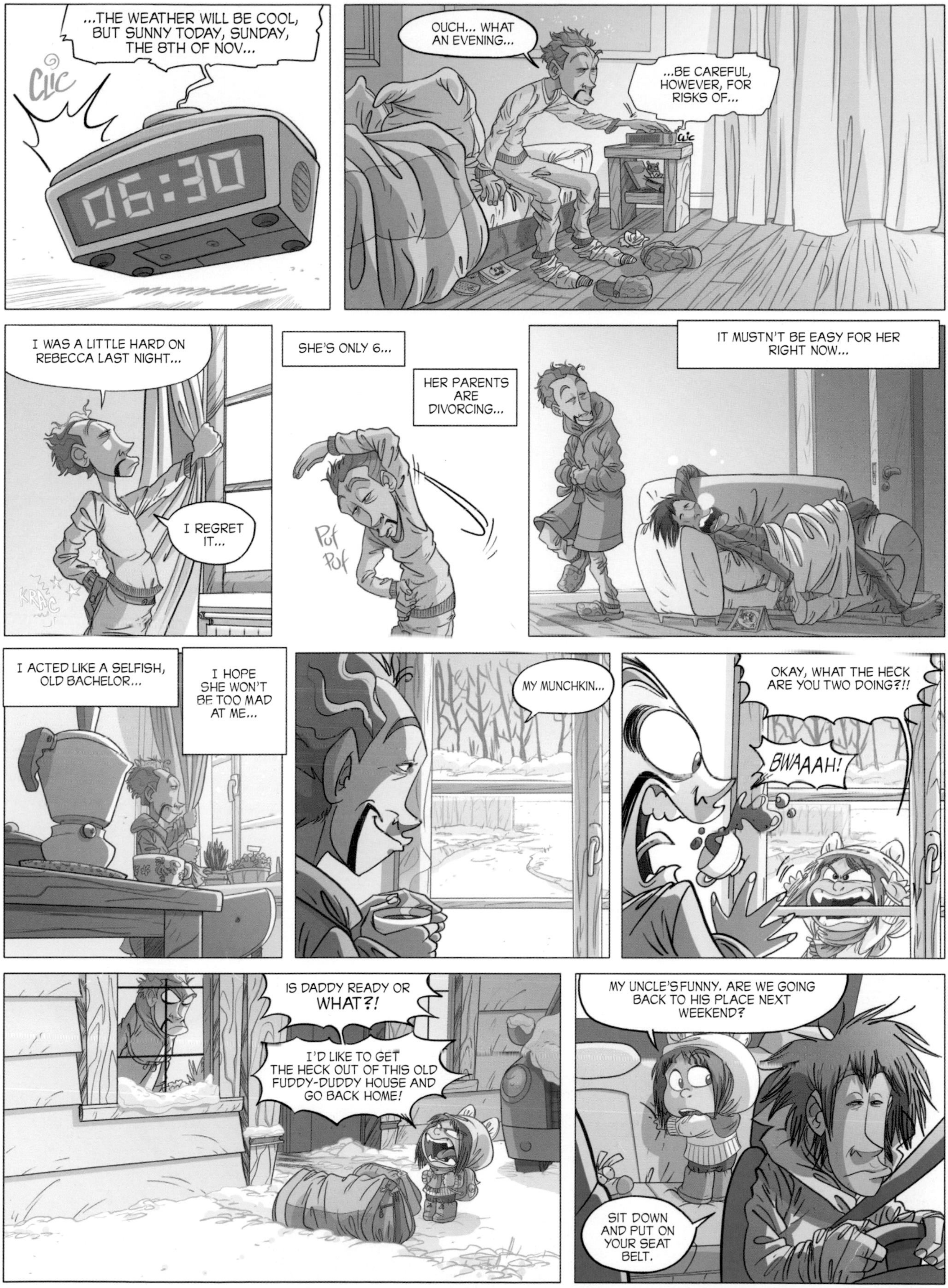
...THE WEATHER WILL BE COOL, BUT SUNNY TODAY, SUNDAY, THE 8TH OF NOV...
CLIC
06:30
OUCH... WHAT AN EVENING...
...BE CAREFUL, HOWEVER, FOR RISKS OF...
CLIC
I WAS A LITTLE HARD ON REBECCA LAST NIGHT...
I REGRET IT...
KRAC
SHE'S ONLY 6...
HER PARENTS ARE DIVORCING...
PUF PUF
IT MUSTN'T BE EASY FOR HER RIGHT NOW...
I ACTED LIKE A SELFISH, OLD BACHELOR...
I HOPE SHE WON'T BE TOO MAD AT ME...
MY MUNCHKIN...
OKAY, WHAT THE HECK ARE YOU TWO DOING?!!
BWAAAH!
IS DADDY READY OR WHAT?!
I'D LIKE TO GET THE HECK OUT OF THIS OLD FUDDY-DUDDY HOUSE AND GO BACK HOME!
MY UNCLE'S FUNNY. ARE WE GOING BACK TO HIS PLACE NEXT WEEKEND?
SIT DOWN AND PUT ON YOUR SEAT BELT.

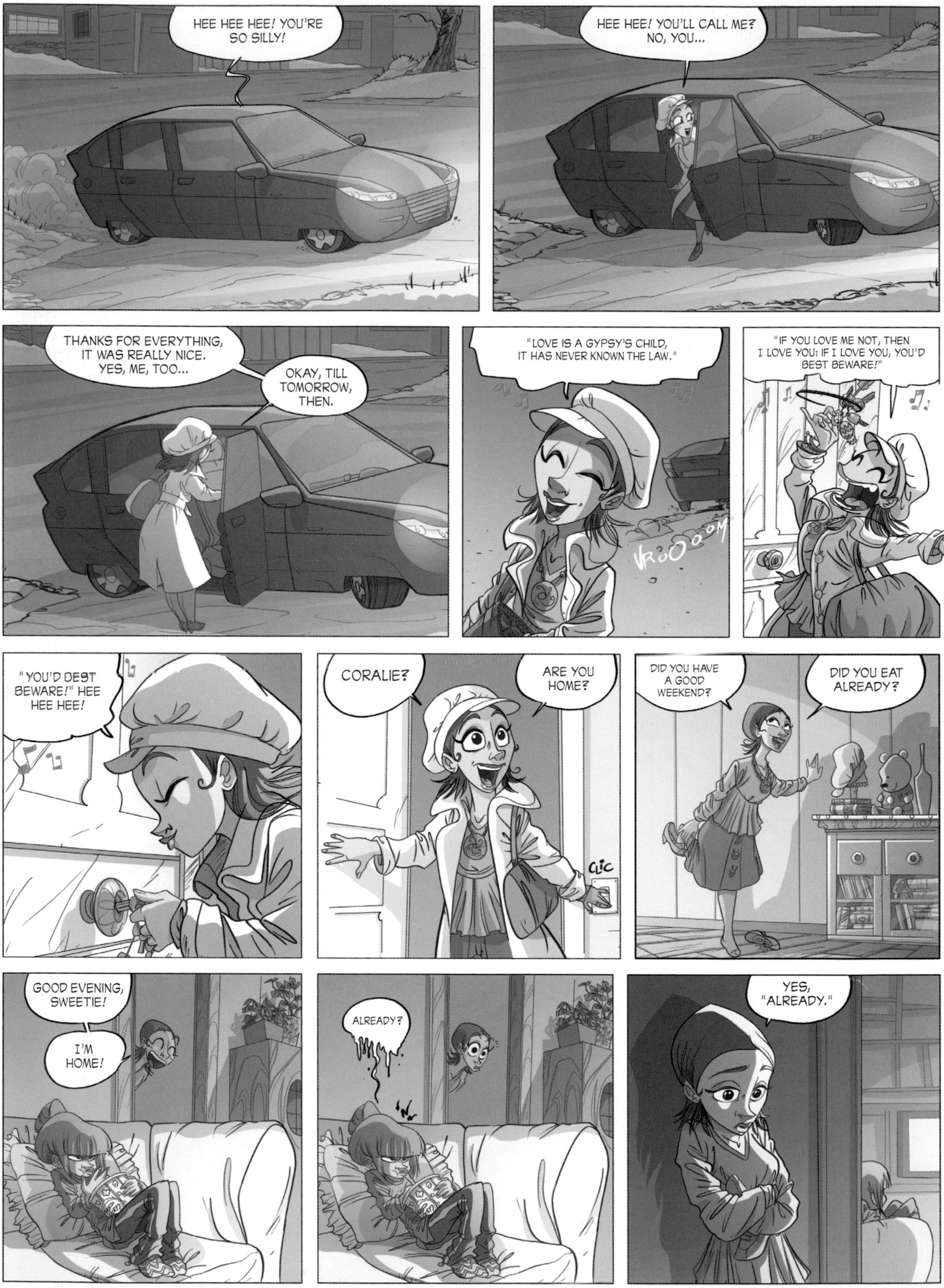

HEE HEE HEE! YOU'RE SO SILLY!
HEE HEE! YOU'LL CALL ME? NO, YOU...
THANKS FOR EVERYTHING, IT WAS REALLY NICE. YES, ME, TOO...
OKAY, TILL TOMORROW, THEN.
"LOVE IS A GYPSY'S CHILD, IT HAS NEVER KNOWN THE LAW."
VROOOOOM
"IF YOU LOVE ME NOT, THEN I LOVE YOU; IF I LOVE YOU, YOU'D BEST BEWARE!"
"YOU'D BEST BEWARE!" HEE HEE HEE!
CORALIE?
ARE YOU HOME?
CLIC
DID YOU HAVE A GOOD WEEKEND?
DID YOU EAT ALREADY?
GOOD EVENING, SWEETIE!
I'M HOME!
ALREADY?
YES, "ALREADY."

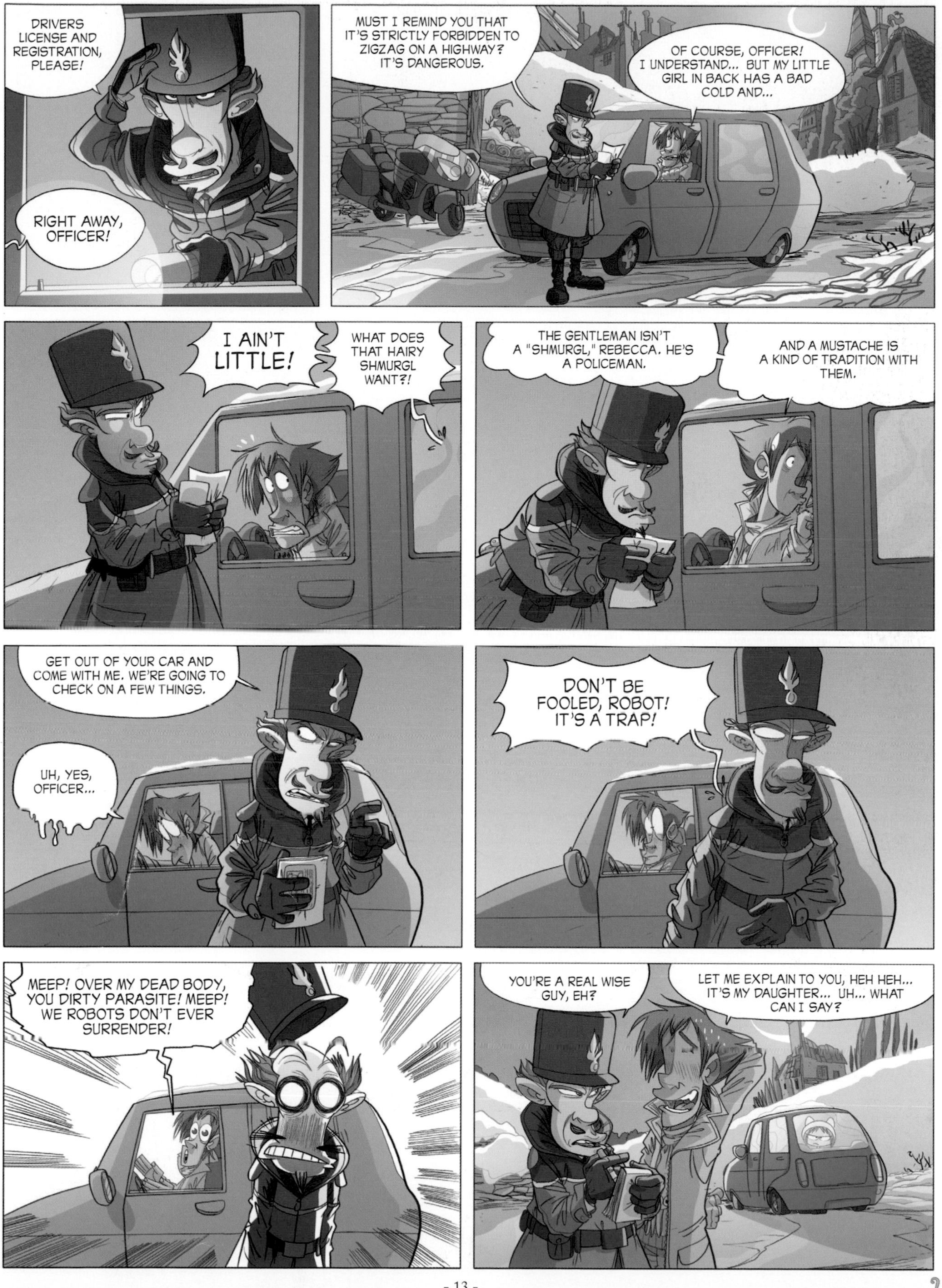
DRIVERS LICENSE AND REGISTRATION, PLEASE!
RIGHT AWAY, OFFICER!
MUST I REMIND YOU THAT IT'S STRICTLY FORBIDDEN TO ZIGZAG ON A HIGHWAY? IT'S DANGEROUS.
OF COURSE, OFFICER! I UNDERSTAND... BUT MY LITTLE GIRL IN BACK HAS A BAD COLD AND...
I AIN'T LITTLE!
WHAT DOES THAT HAIRY SHMURGL WANT?!
THE GENTLEMAN ISN'T A "SHMURGL," REBECCA. HE'S A POLICEMAN.
AND A MUSTACHE IS A KIND OF TRADITION WITH THEM.
GET OUT OF YOUR CAR AND COME WITH ME. WE'RE GOING TO CHECK ON A FEW THINGS.
UH, YES, OFFICER...
DON'T BE FOOLED, ROBOT! IT'S A TRAP!
MEEP! OVER MY DEAD BODY, YOU DIRTY PARASITE! MEEP! WE ROBOTS DON'T EVER SURRENDER!
YOU'RE A REAL WISE GUY, EH?
LET ME EXPLAIN TO YOU, HEH HEH... IT'S MY DAUGHTER... UH... WHAT CAN I SAY?

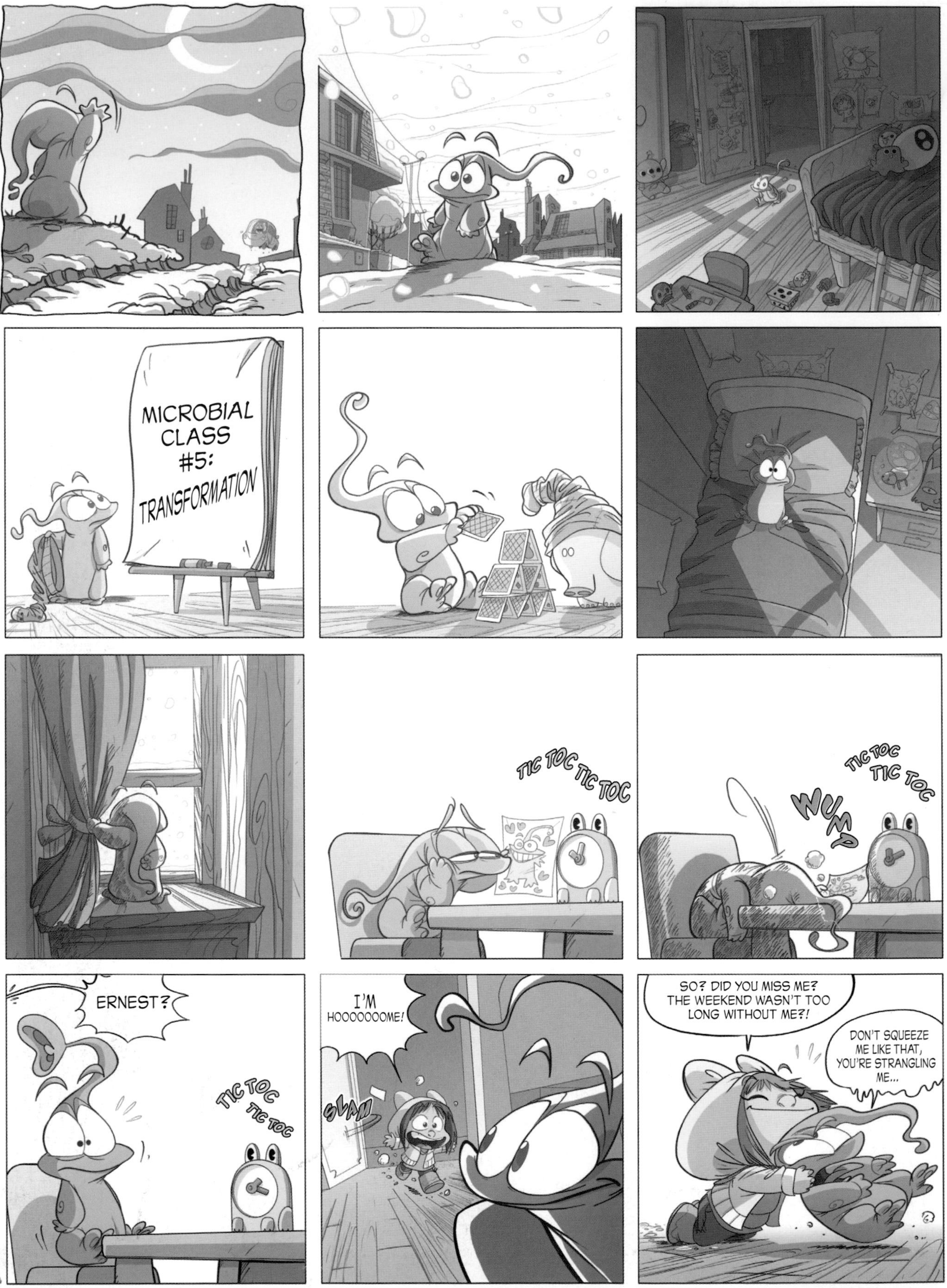
MICROBIAL CLASS #5: TRANSFORMATION
TIC TOC TIC TOC
TIC TOC TIC TOC
WUMP
ERNEST?
TIC TOC TIC TOC
I'M HOOOOOOOME!
SLAM
SO? DID YOU MISS ME? THE WEEKEND WASN'T TOO LONG WITHOUT ME?!
DON'T SQUEEZE ME LIKE THAT, YOU'RE STRANGLING ME...

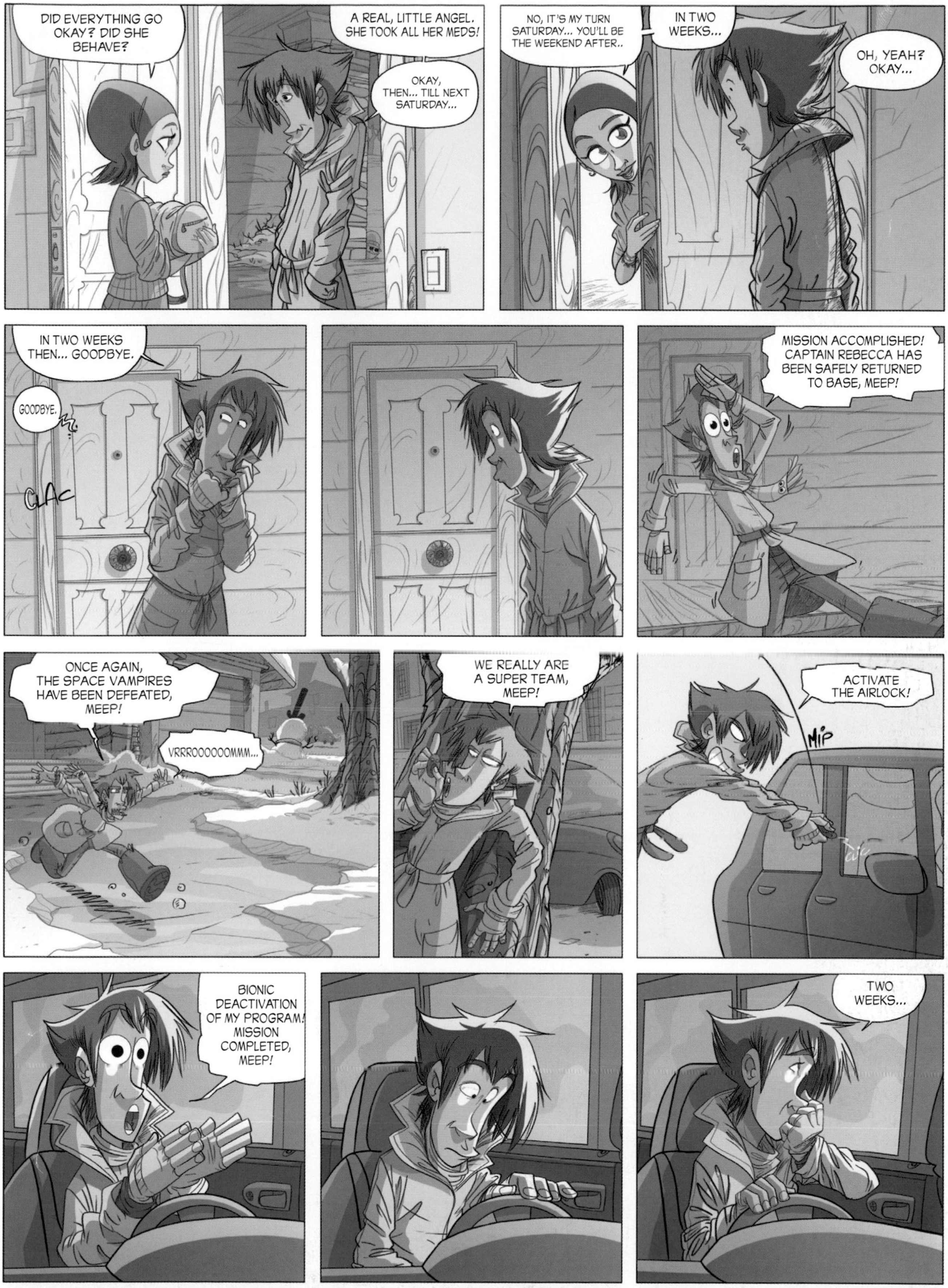
DID EVERYTHING GO OKAY? DID SHE BEHAVE?
A REAL, LITTLE ANGEL. SHE TOOK ALL HER MEDS!
OKAY, THEN... TILL NEXT SATURDAY...
NO, IT'S MY TURN SATURDAY... YOU'LL BE THE WEEKEND AFTER..
IN TWO WEEKS...
OH, YEAH? OKAY...
IN TWO WEEKS THEN... GOODBYE.
GOODBYE.
CLAC
MISSION ACCOMPLISHED! CAPTAIN REBECCA HAS BEEN SAFELY RETURNED TO BASE, MEEP!
ONCE AGAIN, THE SPACE VAMPIRES HAVE BEEN DEFEATED, MEEP!
VRRROOOOOOMMM...
WE REALLY ARE A SUPER TEAM, MEEP!
ACTIVATE THE AIRLOCK!
MIP
BIONIC DEACTIVATION OF MY PROGRAM! MISSION COMPLETED, MEEP!
TWO WEEKS...

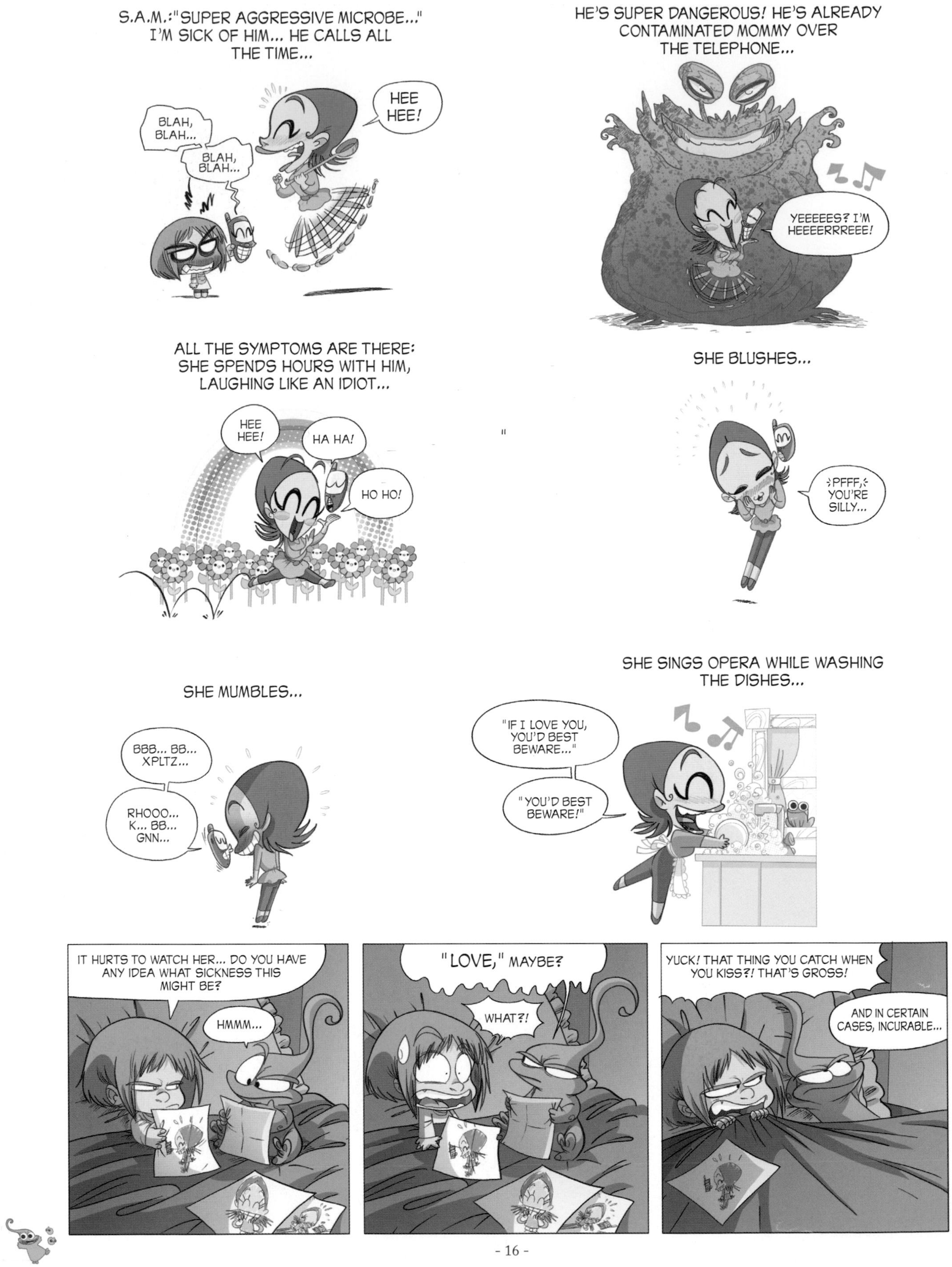

S.A.M.: "SUPER AGGRESSIVE MICROBE..." I'M SICK OF HIM... HE CALLS ALL THE TIME...
BLAH, BLAH...
BLAH, BLAH...
HEE HEE!
HE'S SUPER DANGEROUS! HE'S ALREADY CONTAMINATED MOMMY OVER THE TELEPHONE...
YEEEEES? I'M HEEEERRREEE!
ALL THE SYMPTOMS ARE THERE: SHE SPENDS HOURS WITH HIM, LAUGHING LIKE AN IDIOT...
HEE HEE!
HA HA!
HO HO!
SHE BLUSHES...
PFFF, YOU'RE SILLY...
SHE MUMBLES...
BBB... BB... XPLTZ...
RHOOO... K... BB... GNN...
SHE SINGS OPERA WHILE WASHING THE DISHES...
"IF I LOVE YOU, YOU'D BEST BEWARE..."
"YOU'D BEST BEWARE!"
IT HURTS TO WATCH HER... DO YOU HAVE ANY IDEA WHAT SICKNESS THIS MIGHT BE?
HMMM...
"LOVE," MAYBE?
WHAT?!
YUCK! THAT THING YOU CATCH WHEN YOU KISS?! THAT'S GROSS!
AND IN CERTAIN CASES, INCURABLE...

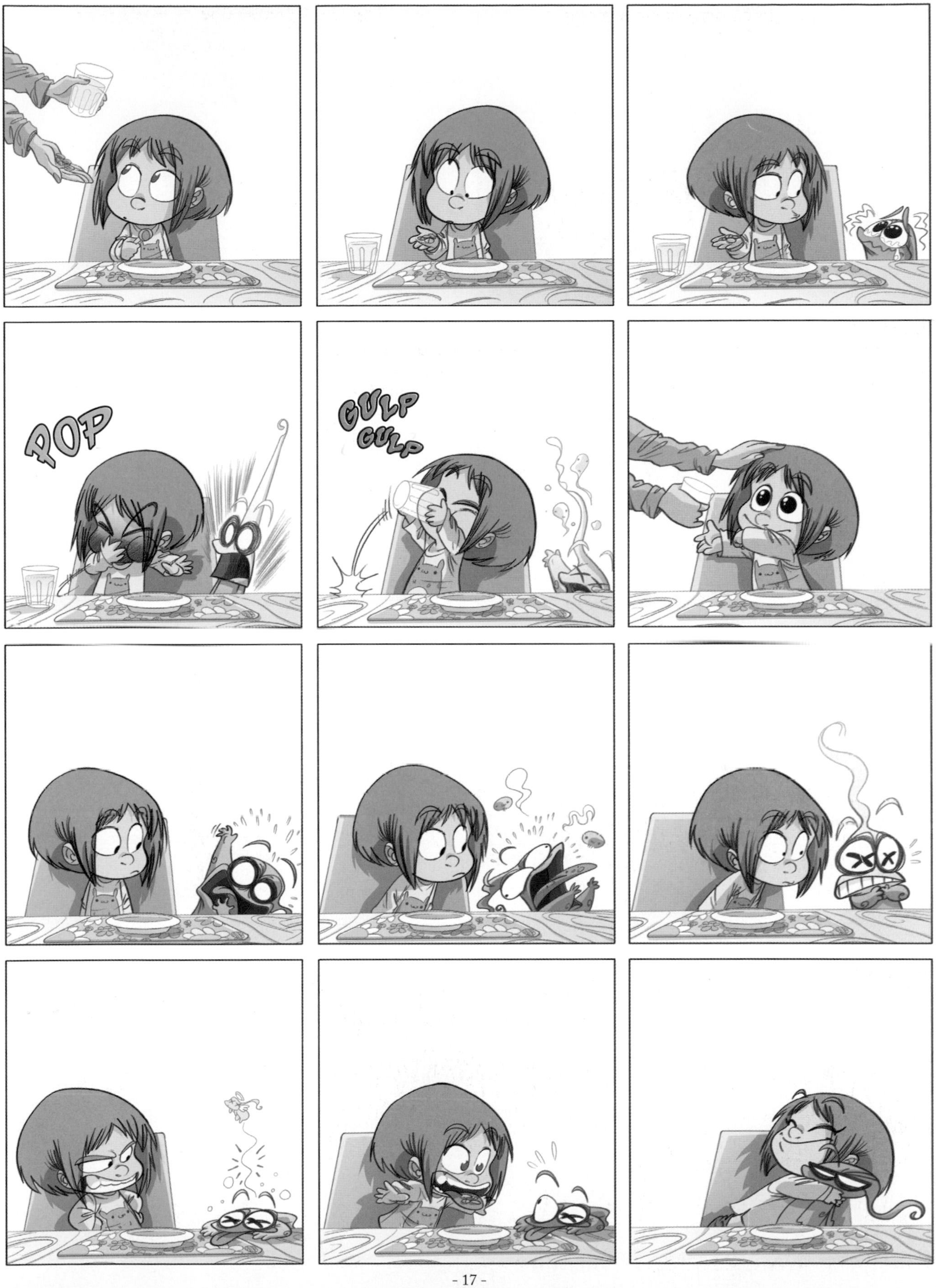
POP
GULP
GULP

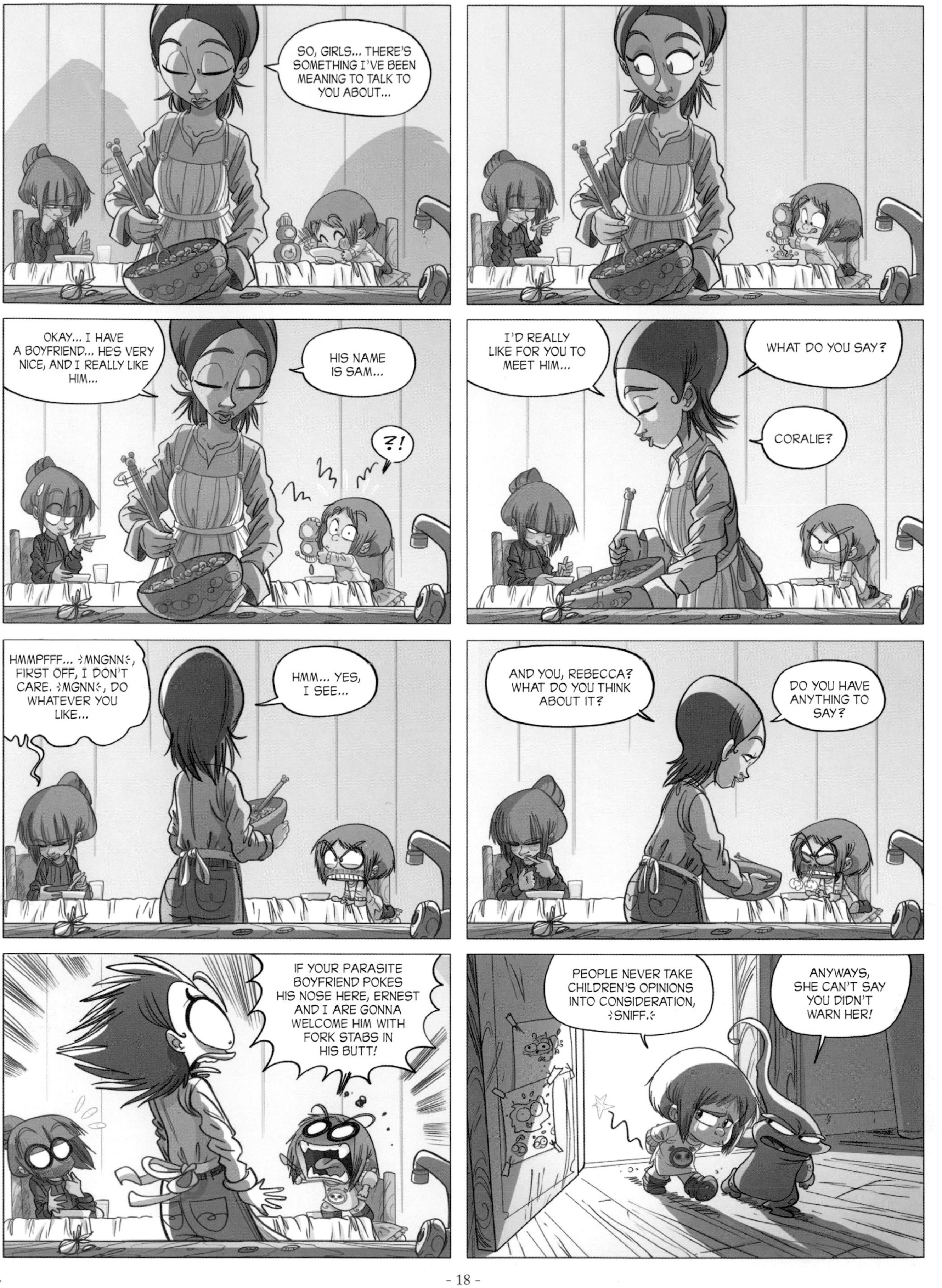
SO, GIRLS... THERE'S SOMETHING I'VE BEEN MEANING TO TALK TO YOU ABOUT...
OKAY... I HAVE A BOYFRIEND... HE'S VERY NICE, AND I REALLY LIKE HIM...
HIS NAME IS SAM...
?!
I'D REALLY LIKE FOR YOU TO MEET HIM...
WHAT DO YOU SAY?
CORALIE?
HMMPFFF... ⊰MNGNN⊱, FIRST OFF, I DON'T CARE. ⊰MGNN⊱, DO WHATEVER YOU LIKE...
HMM... YES, I SEE...
AND YOU, REBECCA? WHAT DO YOU THINK ABOUT IT?
DO YOU HAVE ANYTHING TO SAY?
IF YOUR PARASITE BOYFRIEND POKES HIS NOSE HERE, ERNEST AND I ARE GONNA WELCOME HIM WITH FORK STABS IN HIS BUTT!
PEOPLE NEVER TAKE CHILDREN'S OPINIONS INTO CONSIDERATION, ⊰SNIFF.⊱
ANYWAYS, SHE CAN'T SAY YOU DIDN'T WARN HER!

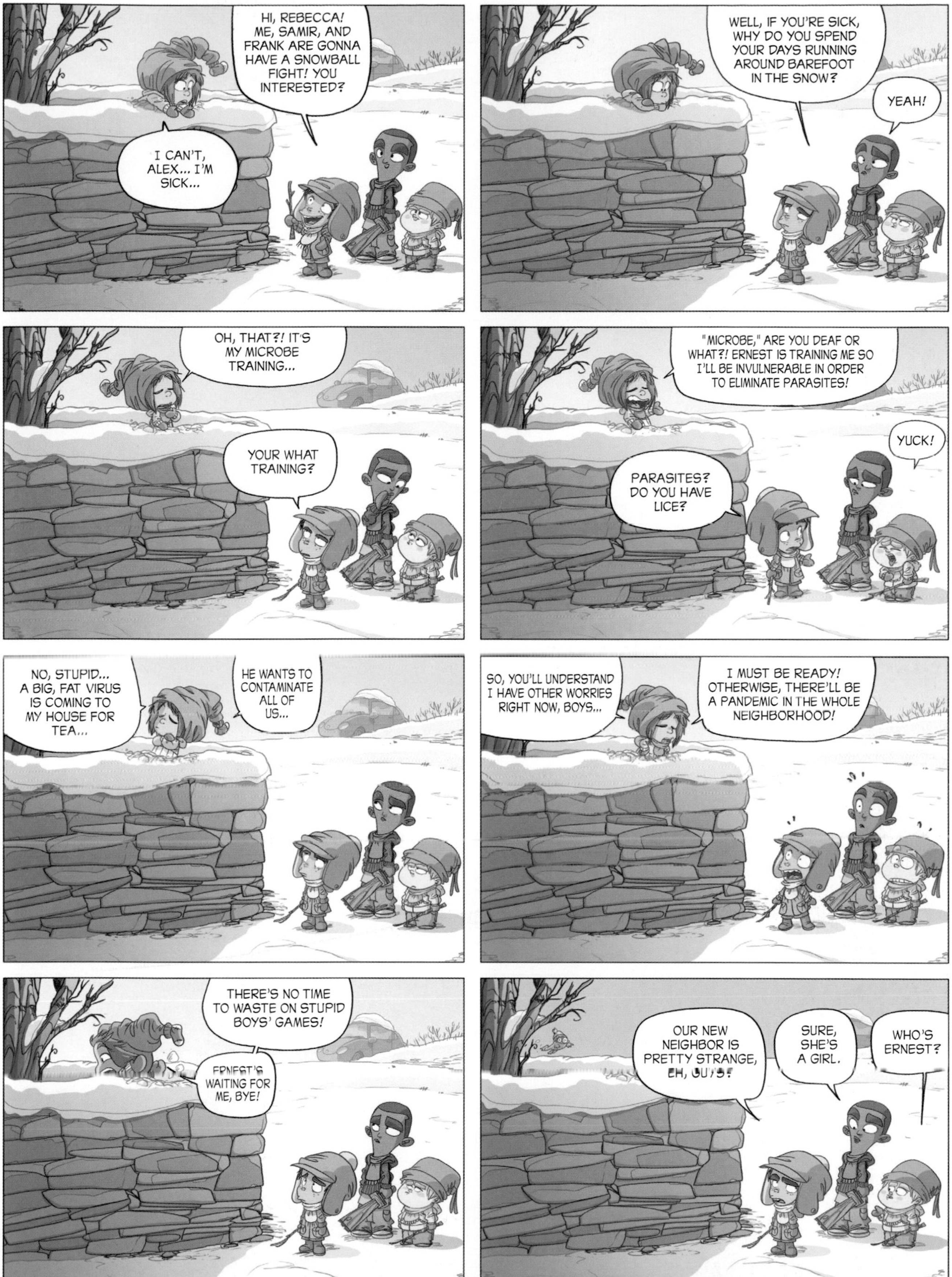
HI, REBECCA! ME, SAMIR, AND FRANK ARE GONNA HAVE A SNOWBALL FIGHT! YOU INTERESTED?
I CAN'T, ALEX... I'M SICK...
WELL, IF YOU'RE SICK, WHY DO YOU SPEND YOUR DAYS RUNNING AROUND BAREFOOT IN THE SNOW?
YEAH!
OH, THAT?! IT'S MY MICROBE TRAINING...
YOUR WHAT TRAINING?
"MICROBE," ARE YOU DEAF OR WHAT?! ERNEST IS TRAINING ME SO I'LL BE INVULNERABLE IN ORDER TO ELIMINATE PARASITES!
PARASITES? DO YOU HAVE LICE?
YUCK!
NO, STUPID... A BIG, FAT VIRUS IS COMING TO MY HOUSE FOR TEA...
HE WANTS TO CONTAMINATE ALL OF US...
SO, YOU'LL UNDERSTAND I HAVE OTHER WORRIES RIGHT NOW, BOYS...
I MUST BE READY! OTHERWISE, THERE'LL BE A PANDEMIC IN THE WHOLE NEIGHBORHOOD!
THERE'S NO TIME TO WASTE ON STUPID BOYS' GAMES!
ERNEST'S WAITING FOR ME, BYE!
OUR NEW NEIGHBOR IS PRETTY STRANGE, EH, GUYS?
SURE, SHE'S A GIRL.
WHO'S ERNEST?

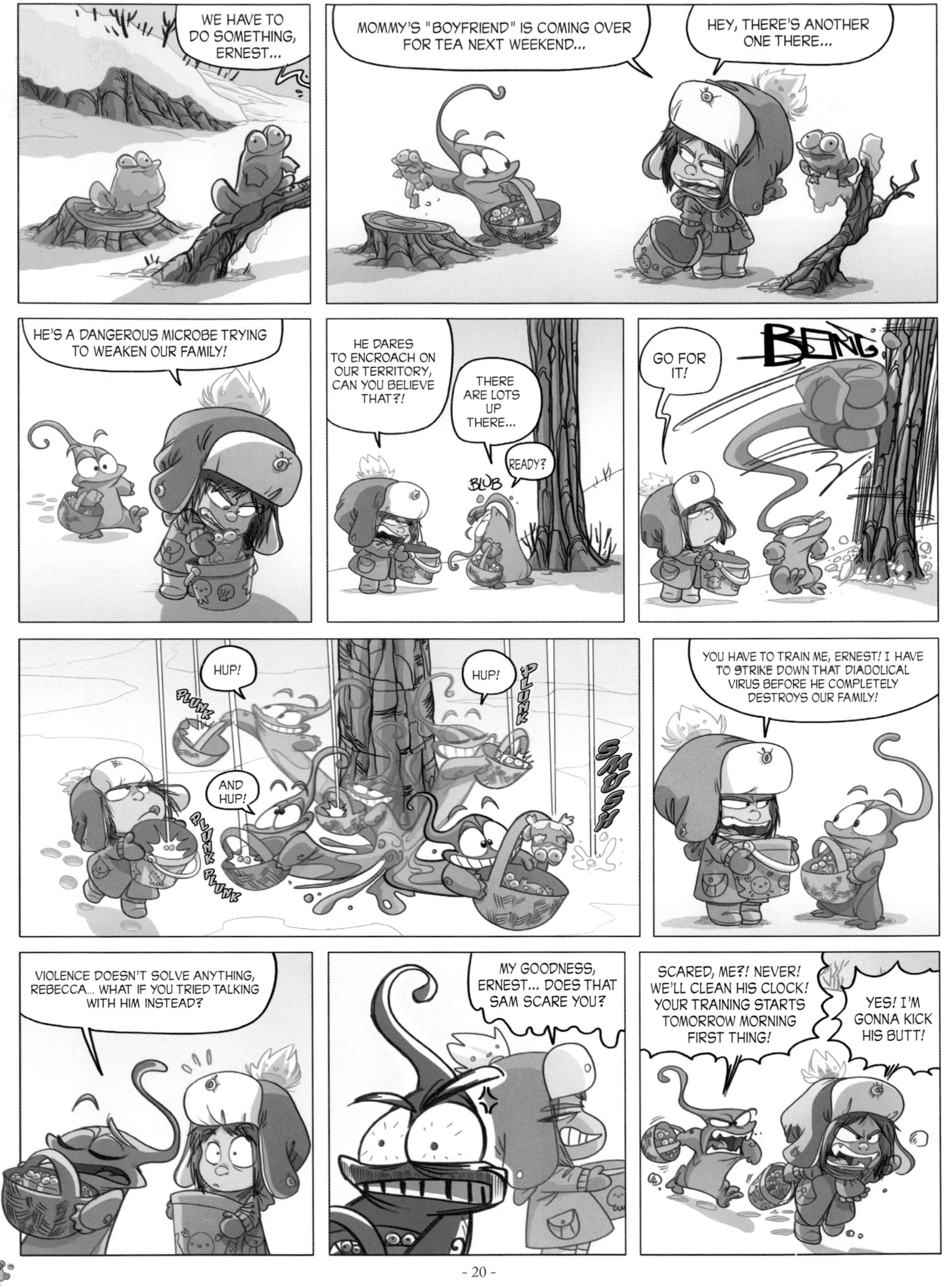
WE HAVE TO DO SOMETHING, ERNEST...
MOMMY'S "BOYFRIEND" IS COMING OVER FOR TEA NEXT WEEKEND...
HEY, THERE'S ANOTHER ONE THERE...
HE'S A DANGEROUS MICROBE TRYING TO WEAKEN OUR FAMILY!
HE DARES TO ENCROACH ON OUR TERRITORY, CAN YOU BELIEVE THAT?!
THERE ARE LOTS UP THERE...
BLUB
READY?
GO FOR IT!
BENG
HUP!
PLUNK
HUP!
PLUNK
AND HUP!
PLUNK PLUNK
SMUSH
YOU HAVE TO TRAIN ME, ERNEST! I HAVE TO STRIKE DOWN THAT DIABOLICAL VIRUS BEFORE HE COMPLETELY DESTROYS OUR FAMILY!
VIOLENCE DOESN'T SOLVE ANYTHING, REBECCA... WHAT IF YOU TRIED TALKING WITH HIM INSTEAD?
MY GOODNESS, ERNEST... DOES THAT SAM SCARE YOU?
SCARED, ME?! NEVER! WE'LL CLEAN HIS CLOCK! YOUR TRAINING STARTS TOMORROW MORNING FIRST THING!
YES! I'M GONNA KICK HIS BUTT!

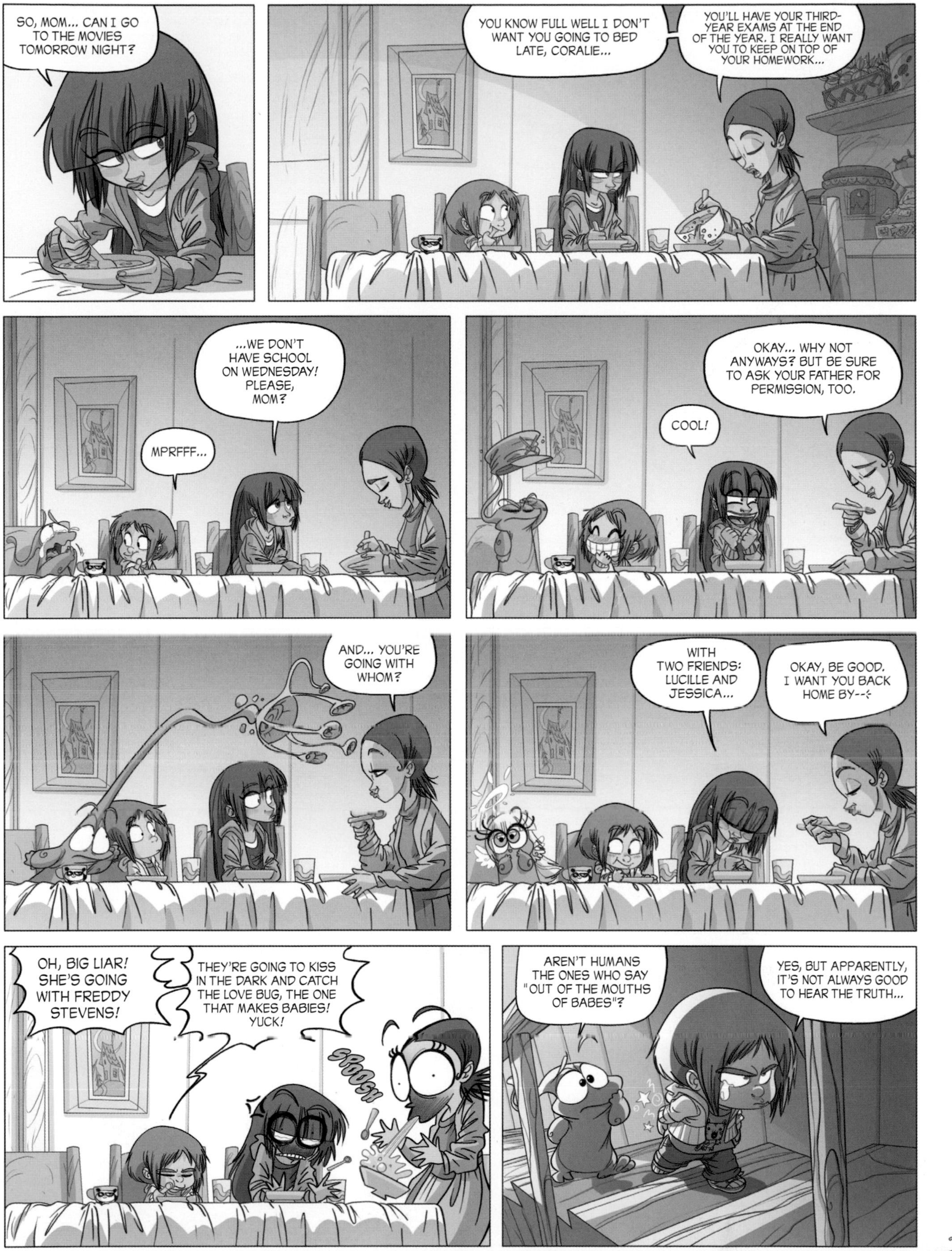
SO, MOM... CAN I GO TO THE MOVIES TOMORROW NIGHT?
YOU KNOW FULL WELL I DON'T WANT YOU GOING TO BED LATE, CORALIE...
YOU'LL HAVE YOUR THIRD-YEAR EXAMS AT THE END OF THE YEAR. I REALLY WANT YOU TO KEEP ON TOP OF YOUR HOMEWORK...
...WE DON'T HAVE SCHOOL ON WEDNESDAY! PLEASE, MOM?
MPRFFF...
OKAY... WHY NOT ANYWAYS? BUT BE SURE TO ASK YOUR FATHER FOR PERMISSION, TOO.
COOL!
AND... YOU'RE GOING WITH WHOM?
WITH TWO FRIENDS: LUCILLE AND JESSICA...
OKAY, BE GOOD. I WANT YOU BACK HOME BY--
OH, BIG LIAR! SHE'S GOING WITH FREDDY STEVENS!
THEY'RE GOING TO KISS IN THE DARK AND CATCH THE LOVE BUG, THE ONE THAT MAKES BABIES! YUCK!
SPLOOSH
AREN'T HUMANS THE ONES WHO SAY "OUT OF THE MOUTHS OF BABES"?
YES, BUT APPARENTLY, IT'S NOT ALWAYS GOOD TO HEAR THE TRUTH...

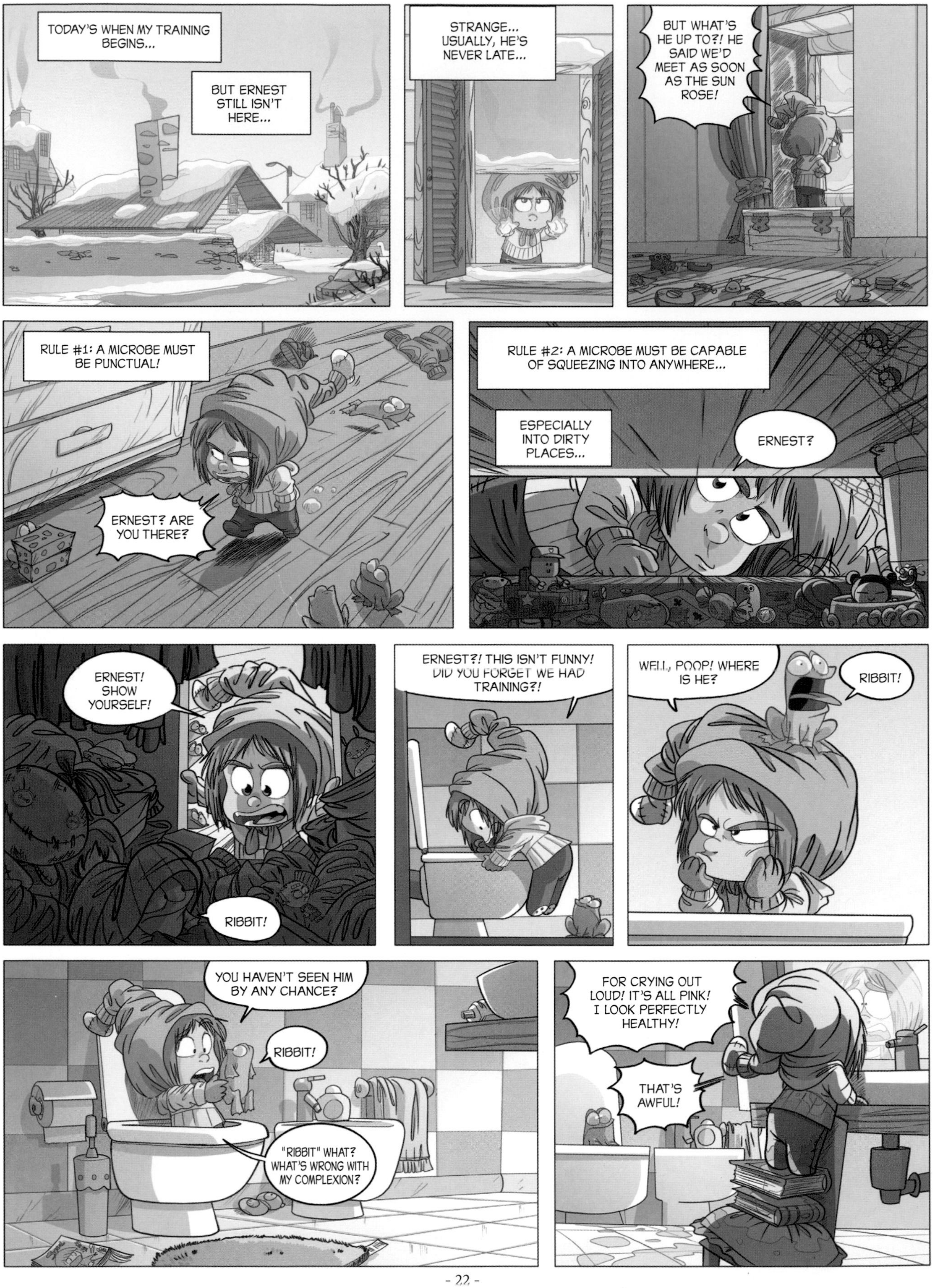
TODAY'S WHEN MY TRAINING BEGINS...
BUT ERNEST STILL ISN'T HERE...
STRANGE... USUALLY, HE'S NEVER LATE...
BUT WHAT'S HE UP TO?! HE SAID WE'D MEET AS SOON AS THE SUN ROSE!
RULE #1: A MICROBE MUST BE PUNCTUAL!
ERNEST? ARE YOU THERE?
RULE #2: A MICROBE MUST BE CAPABLE OF SQUEEZING INTO ANYWHERE...
ESPECIALLY INTO DIRTY PLACES...
ERNEST?
ERNEST! SHOW YOURSELF!
RIBBIT!
ERNEST?! THIS ISN'T FUNNY! DID YOU FORGET WE HAD TRAINING?!
WELL, POOP! WHERE IS HE?
RIBBIT!
YOU HAVEN'T SEEN HIM BY ANY CHANCE?
RIBBIT!
"RIBBIT" WHAT? WHAT'S WRONG WITH MY COMPLEXION?
FOR CRYING OUT LOUD! IT'S ALL PINK! I LOOK PERFECTLY HEALTHY!
THAT'S AWFUL!

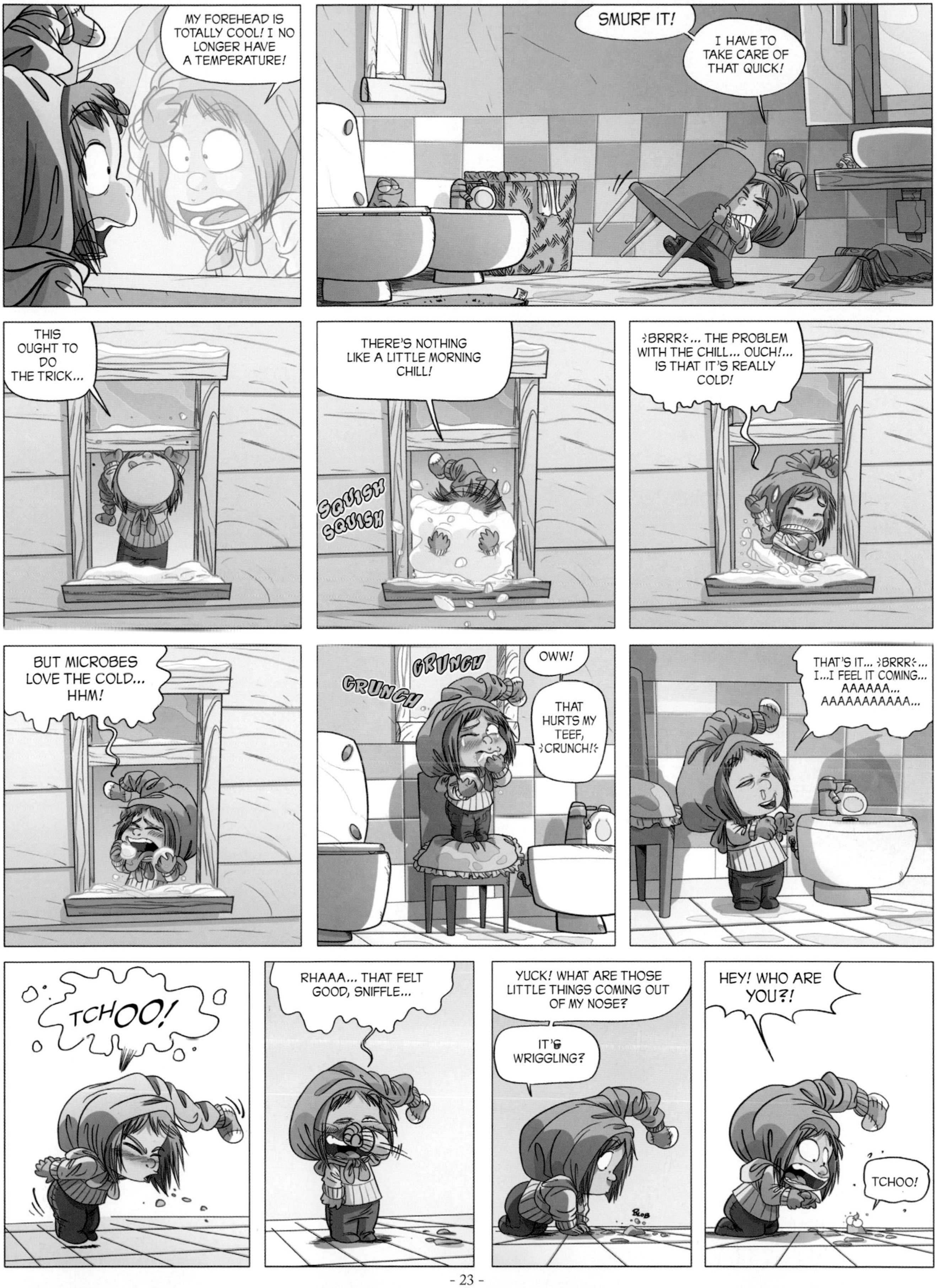
MY FOREHEAD IS TOTALLY COOL! I NO LONGER HAVE A TEMPERATURE!
SMURF IT!
I HAVE TO TAKE CARE OF THAT QUICK!
THIS OUGHT TO DO THE TRICK...
THERE'S NOTHING LIKE A LITTLE MORNING CHILL!
SQUISH
SQUISH
›BRRR‹... THE PROBLEM WITH THE CHILL... OUCH!... IS THAT IT'S REALLY COLD!
BUT MICROBES LOVE THE COLD... HHM!
CRUNCH
CRUNCH
OWW!
THAT HURTS MY TEEF, ›CRUNCH!‹
THAT'S IT... ›BRRR‹... I...I FEEL IT COMING... AAAAAA... AAAAAAAAAAA...
TCHOO!
RHAAA... THAT FELT GOOD, SNIFFLE...
YUCK! WHAT ARE THOSE LITTLE THINGS COMING OUT OF MY NOSE?
IT'S WRIGGLING?
HEY! WHO ARE YOU?!
TCHOO!

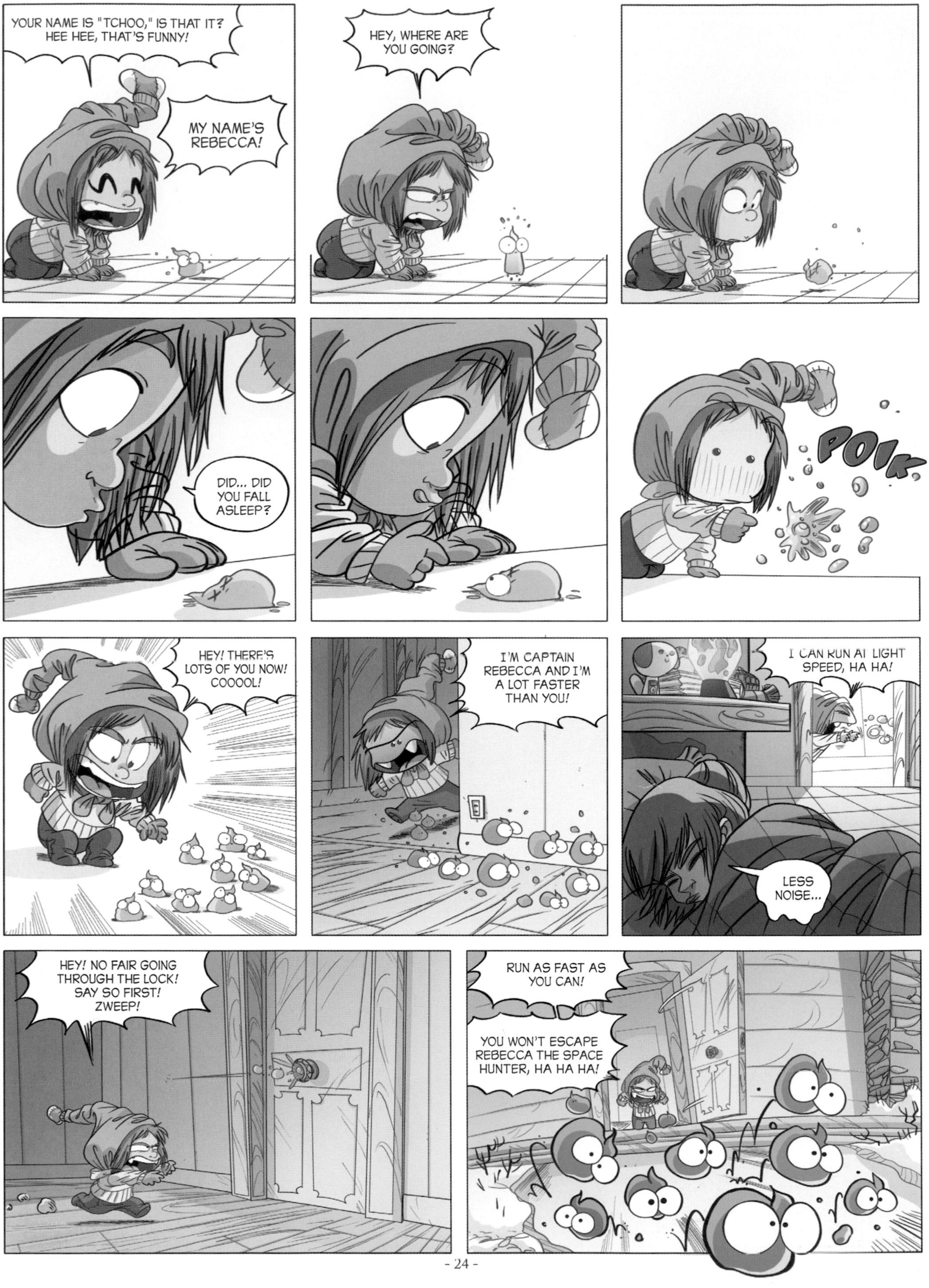

YOUR NAME IS "TCHOO," IS THAT IT? HEE HEE, THAT'S FUNNY!
MY NAME'S REBECCA!
HEY, WHERE ARE YOU GOING?
DID... DID YOU FALL ASLEEP?
POIK
HEY! THERE'S LOTS OF YOU NOW! COOOOL!
I'M CAPTAIN REBECCA AND I'M A LOT FASTER THAN YOU!
I CAN RUN AT LIGHT SPEED, HA HA!
LESS NOISE...
HEY! NO FAIR GOING THROUGH THE LOCK! SAY SO FIRST! ZWEEP!
RUN AS FAST AS YOU CAN!
YOU WON'T ESCAPE REBECCA THE SPACE HUNTER, HA HA HA!

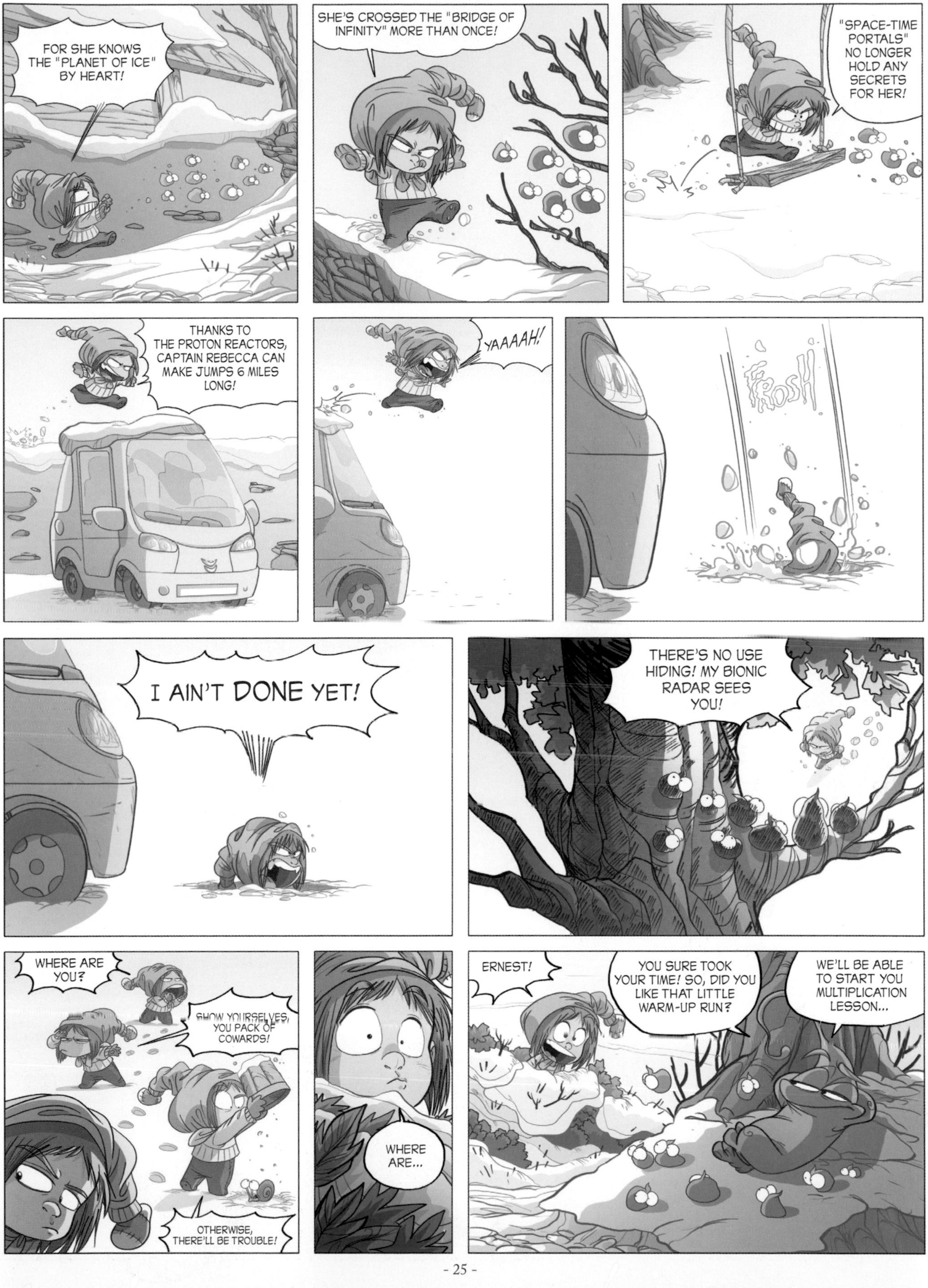

FOR SHE KNOWS THE "PLANET OF ICE" BY HEART!
SHE'S CROSSED THE "BRIDGE OF INFINITY" MORE THAN ONCE!
"SPACE-TIME PORTALS" NO LONGER HOLD ANY SECRETS FOR HER!
THANKS TO THE PROTON REACTORS, CAPTAIN REBECCA CAN MAKE JUMPS 6 MILES LONG!
YAAAAH!
FROSH
I AIN'T DONE YET!
THERE'S NO USE HIDING! MY BIONIC RADAR SEES YOU!
WHERE ARE YOU?
SHOW YOURSELVES, YOU PACK OF COWARDS!
OTHERWISE, THERE'LL BE TROUBLE!
WHERE ARE...
ERNEST!
YOU SURE TOOK YOUR TIME! SO, DID YOU LIKE THAT LITTLE WARM-UP RUN?
WE'LL BE ABLE TO START YOU MULTIPLICATION LESSON...

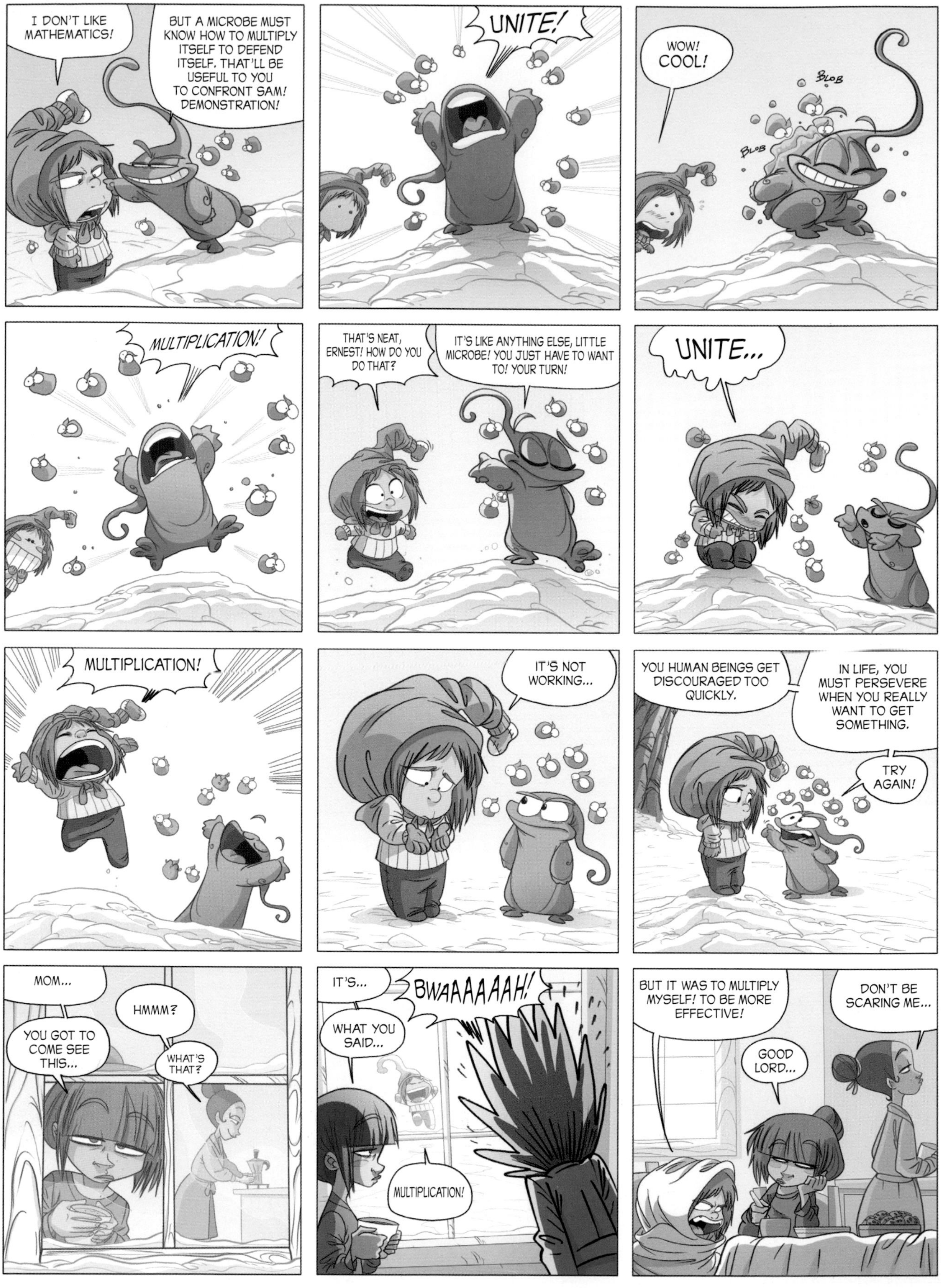
I DON'T LIKE MATHEMATICS!
BUT A MICROBE MUST KNOW HOW TO MULTIPLY ITSELF TO DEFEND ITSELF. THAT'LL BE USEFUL TO YOU TO CONFRONT SAM! DEMONSTRATION!
UNITE!
WOW! COOL!
BLOB
BLOB
MULTIPLICATION!
THAT'S NEAT, ERNEST! HOW DO YOU DO THAT?
IT'S LIKE ANYTHING ELSE, LITTLE MICROBE! YOU JUST HAVE TO WANT TO! YOUR TURN!
UNITE...
MULTIPLICATION!
IT'S NOT WORKING...
YOU HUMAN BEINGS GET DISCOURAGED TOO QUICKLY.
IN LIFE, YOU MUST PERSEVERE WHEN YOU REALLY WANT TO GET SOMETHING.
TRY AGAIN!
MOM...
HMMM?
YOU GOT TO COME SEE THIS...
WHAT'S THAT?
IT'S...
BWAAAAAAH!
WHAT YOU SAID...
MULTIPLICATION!
BUT IT WAS TO MULTIPLY MYSELF! TO BE MORE EFFECTIVE!
DON'T BE SCARING ME...
GOOD LORD...

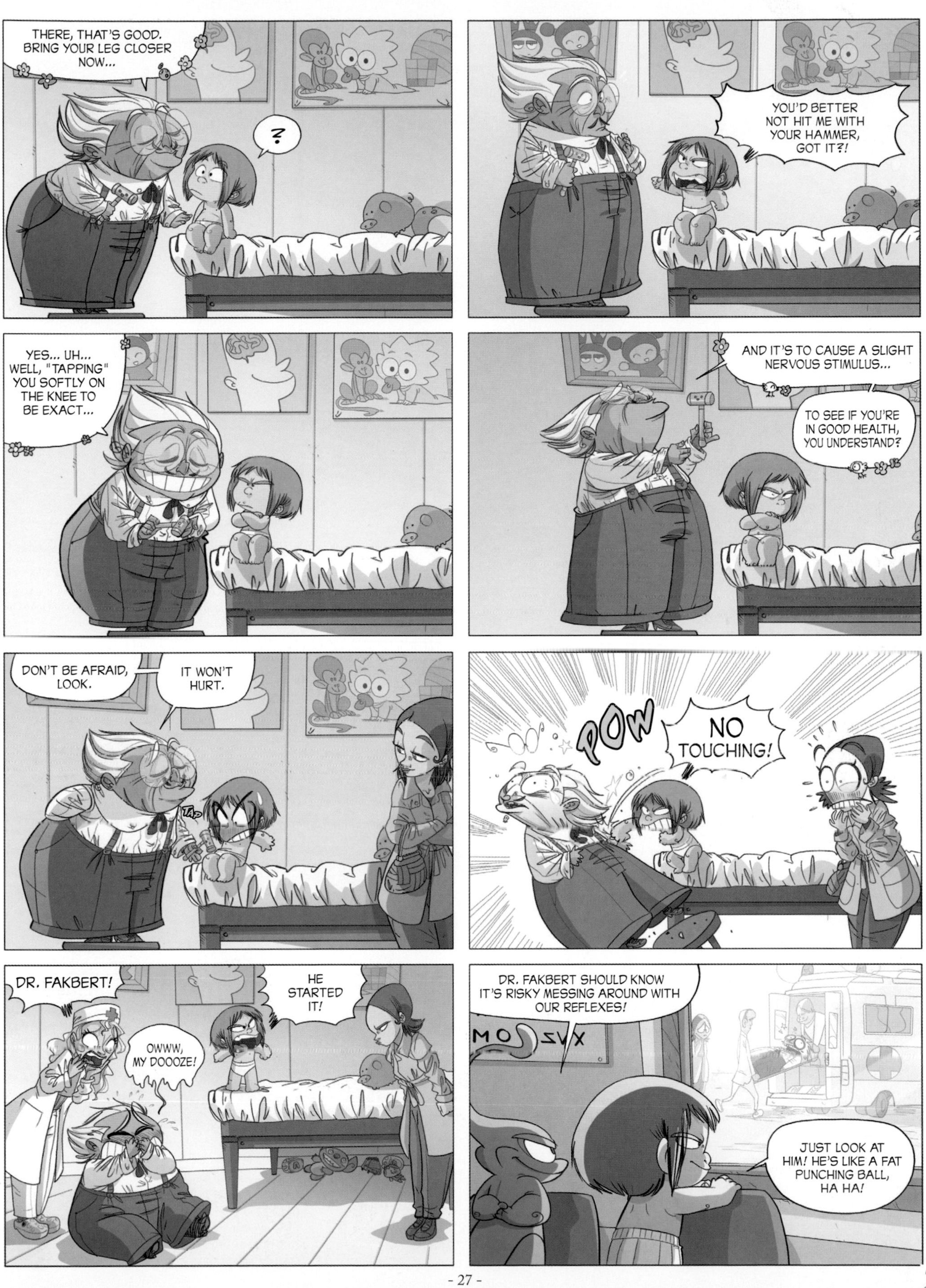
THERE, THAT'S GOOD. BRING YOUR LEG CLOSER NOW...
?
YOU'D BETTER NOT HIT ME WITH YOUR HAMMER, GOT IT?!
YES... UH... WELL, "TAPPING" YOU SOFTLY ON THE KNEE TO BE EXACT...
AND IT'S TO CAUSE A SLIGHT NERVOUS STIMULUS...
TO SEE IF YOU'RE IN GOOD HEALTH, YOU UNDERSTAND?
DON'T BE AFRAID, LOOK.
IT WON'T HURT.
TAP
POW
NO TOUCHING!
DR. FAKBERT!
HE STARTED IT!
OWWW, MY DOOOZE!
DR. FAKBERT SHOULD KNOW IT'S RISKY MESSING AROUND WITH OUR REFLEXES!
JUST LOOK AT HIM! HE'S LIKE A FAT PUNCHING BALL, HA HA!

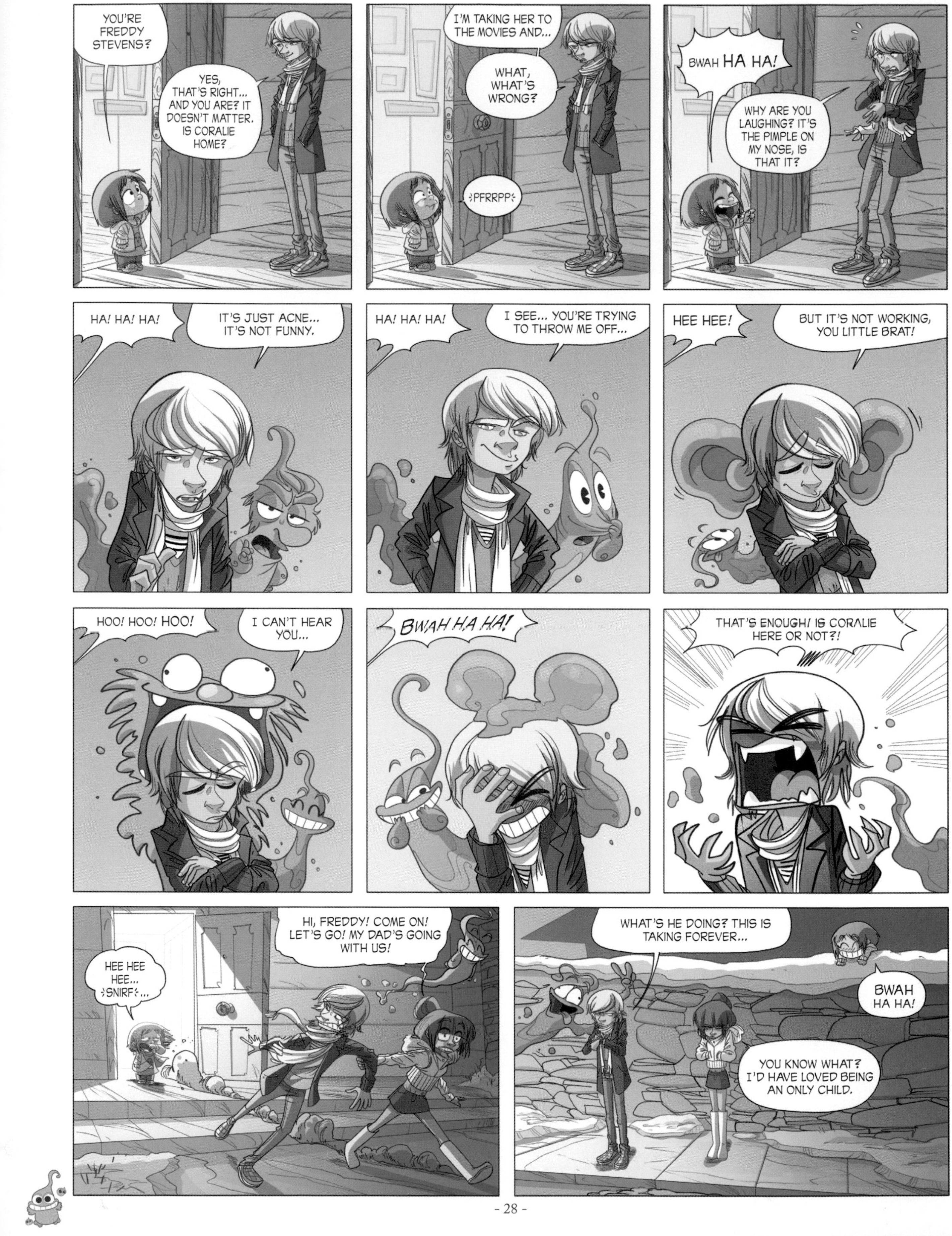
YOU'RE FREDDY STEVENS?
YES, THAT'S RIGHT... AND YOU ARE? IT DOESN'T MATTER. IS CORALIE HOME?
I'M TAKING HER TO THE MOVIES AND...
PFRRPP
WHAT, WHAT'S WRONG?
BWAH HA HA!
WHY ARE YOU LAUGHING? IT'S THE PIMPLE ON MY NOSE, IS THAT IT?
HA! HA! HA!
IT'S JUST ACNE... IT'S NOT FUNNY.
HA! HA! HA!
I SEE... YOU'RE TRYING TO THROW ME OFF...
HEE HEE!
BUT IT'S NOT WORKING, YOU LITTLE BRAT!
HOO! HOO! HOO!
I CAN'T HEAR YOU...
BWAH HA HA!
THAT'S ENOUGH! IS CORALIE HERE OR NOT?!
HEE HEE HEE... SNIRF...
HI, FREDDY! COME ON! LET'S GO! MY DAD'S GOING WITH US!
WHAT'S HE DOING? THIS IS TAKING FOREVER...
BWAH HA HA!
YOU KNOW WHAT? I'D HAVE LOVED BEING AN ONLY CHILD.

I'M GOING TO LOAN YOU A DROP OF PROTOZOAN CELL MATTER...

BLOB

OF WHAT? "PROTOZOAN"?

WE CALL THAT "SYMBIOSIS"!

COOOOOOL...

I'M SURE YOU'LL LIKE IT!

PLOC

HEE HEE! IT'S COLD!

THIS PROTECTIVE MEMBRANE WILL INCREASE YOUR STRENGTH TENFOLD.

YEAH!

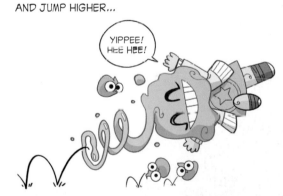

FROM NOW ON, THANKS TO IT, YOU'LL BE ABLE TO SEE FARTHER...

AND JUMP HIGHER...

YIPPEE! HEE HEE!

IN SHORT, IT'LL BE A USEFUL WEAPON TO FIGHT AGAINST PARASITES!

BRING IT ON, SAM!

REBECCA? YOU HAVEN'T SEEN MY PANTYHOSE, BY ANY CHANCE?

THE ONES I BOUGHT LAST WEDNESDAY?

YOUR PANTYHOSE? WHAT PANTYHOSE?

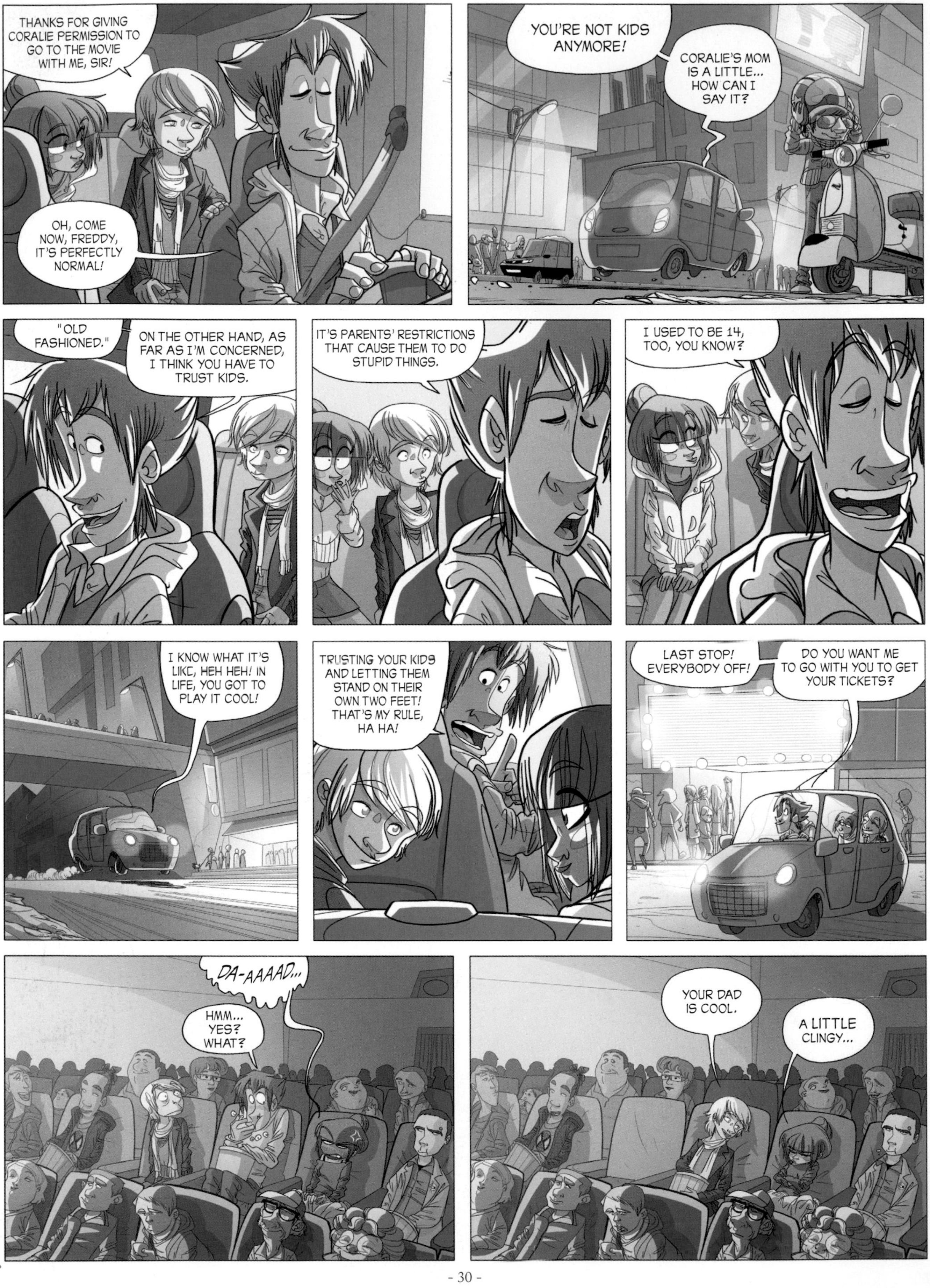

THANKS FOR GIVING CORALIE PERMISSION TO GO TO THE MOVIE WITH ME, SIR!
OH, COME NOW, FREDDY, IT'S PERFECTLY NORMAL!
YOU'RE NOT KIDS ANYMORE!
CORALIE'S MOM IS A LITTLE... HOW CAN I SAY IT?
"OLD FASHIONED."
ON THE OTHER HAND, AS FAR AS I'M CONCERNED, I THINK YOU HAVE TO TRUST KIDS.
IT'S PARENTS' RESTRICTIONS THAT CAUSE THEM TO DO STUPID THINGS.
I USED TO BE 14, TOO, YOU KNOW?
I KNOW WHAT IT'S LIKE, HEH HEH! IN LIFE, YOU GOT TO PLAY IT COOL!
TRUSTING YOUR KIDS AND LETTING THEM STAND ON THEIR OWN TWO FEET! THAT'S MY RULE, HA HA!
LAST STOP! EVERYBODY OFF!
DO YOU WANT ME TO GO WITH YOU TO GET YOUR TICKETS?
DA-AAAAD...
HMM... YES? WHAT?
YOUR DAD IS COOL.
A LITTLE CLINGY...

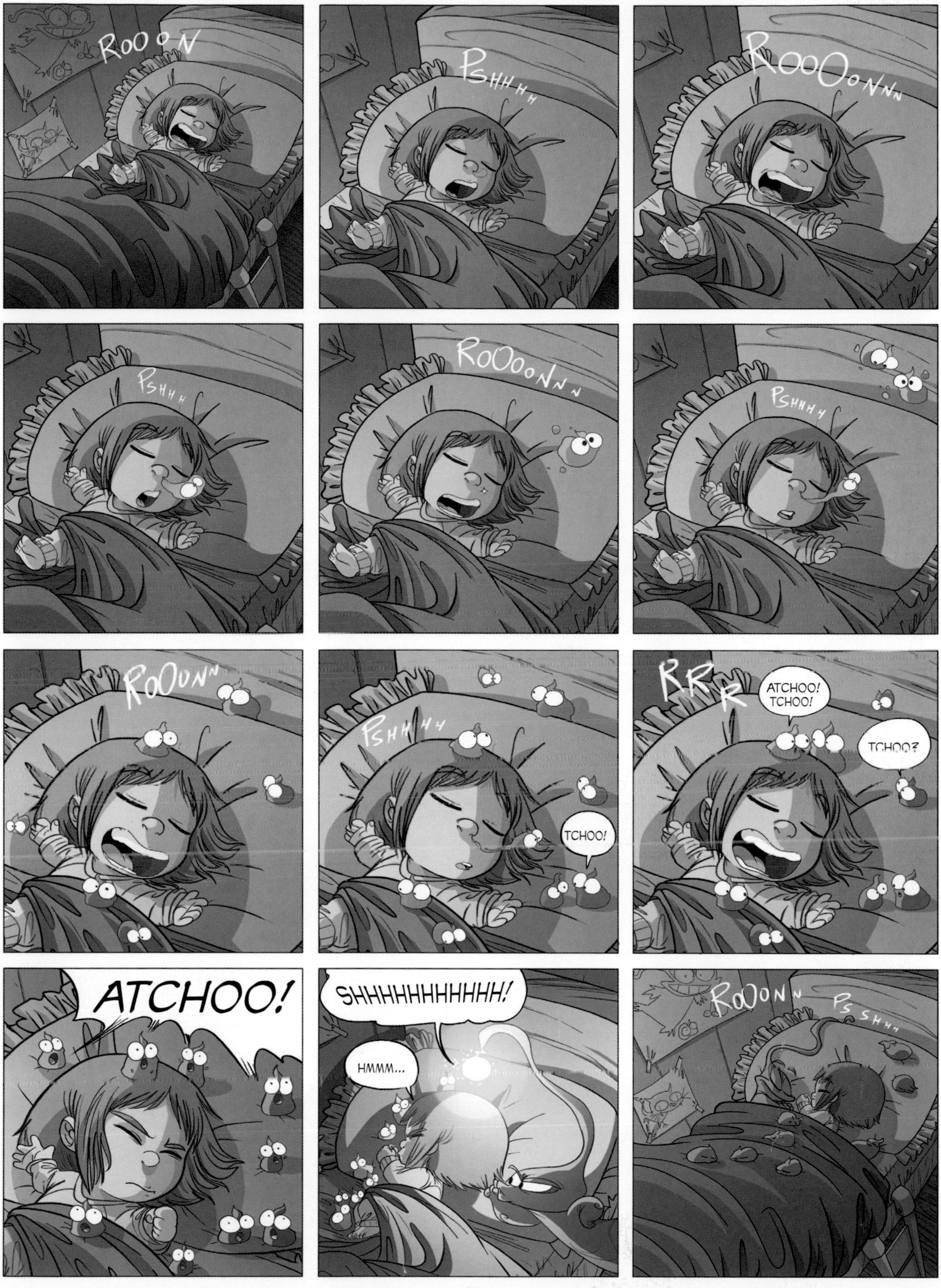
ROOON
PSHHHH
ROOOOONNN
PSHHH
ROOOOONNN
PSHHHH
ROOUNN
PSHHHHH
TCHOO!
RRR
ATCHOO! TCHOO!
TCHOO?
ATCHOO!
SHHHHHHHHHHH!
HMMM...
ROOONN
PSSHHH

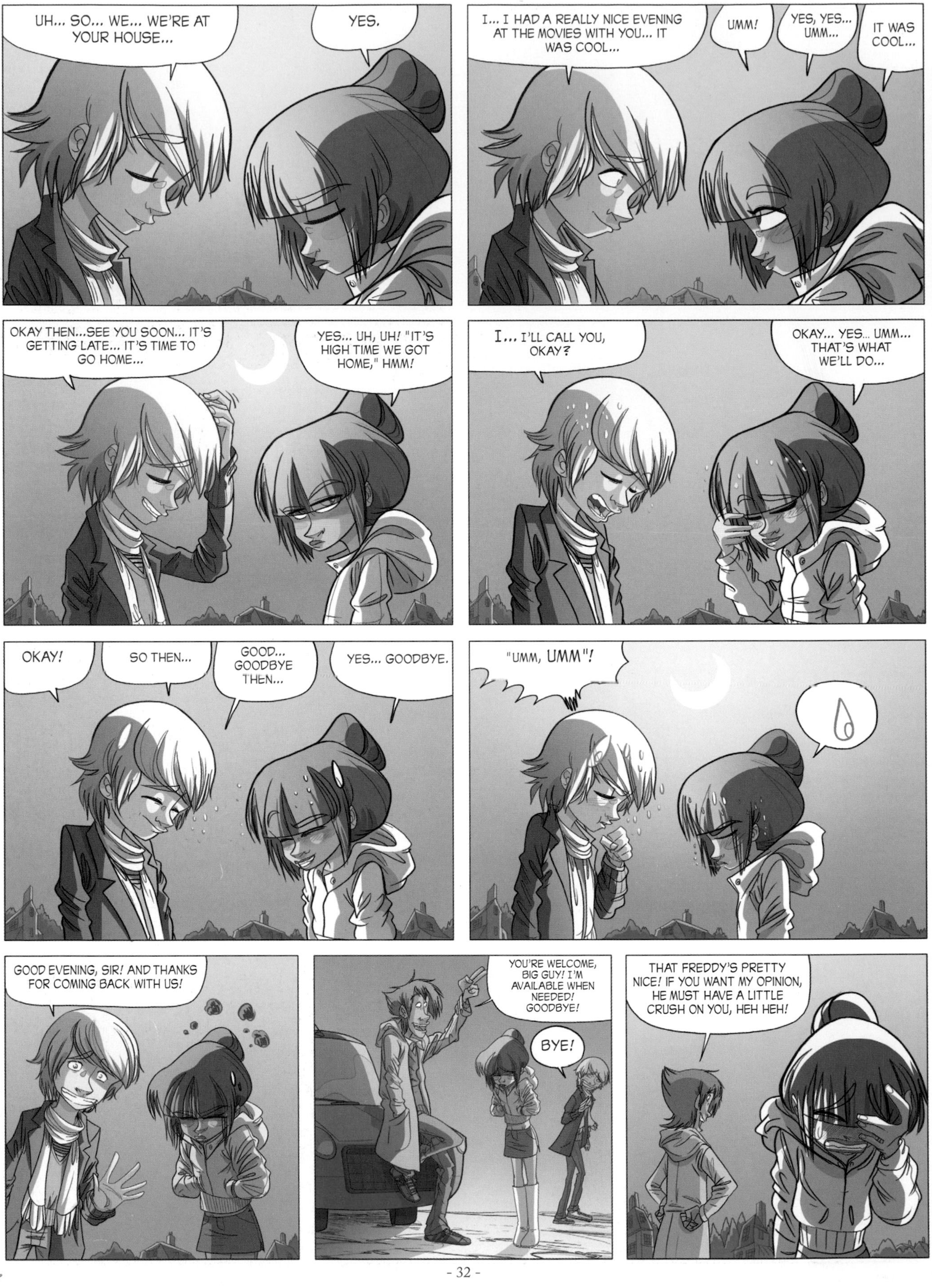
UH... SO... WE... WE'RE AT YOUR HOUSE...
YES.
I... I HAD A REALLY NICE EVENING AT THE MOVIES WITH YOU... IT WAS COOL...
UMM!
YES, YES... UMM...
IT WAS COOL...
OKAY THEN...SEE YOU SOON... IT'S GETTING LATE... IT'S TIME TO GO HOME...
YES... UH, UH! "IT'S HIGH TIME WE GOT HOME," HMM!
I... I'LL CALL YOU, OKAY?
OKAY... YES... UMM... THAT'S WHAT WE'LL DO...
OKAY!
SO THEN...
GOOD... GOODBYE THEN...
YES... GOODBYE.
"UMM, UMM"!
GOOD EVENING, SIR! AND THANKS FOR COMING BACK WITH US!
YOU'RE WELCOME, BIG GUY! I'M AVAILABLE WHEN NEEDED! GOODBYE!
BYE!
THAT FREDDY'S PRETTY NICE! IF YOU WANT MY OPINION, HE MUST HAVE A LITTLE CRUSH ON YOU, HEH HEH!

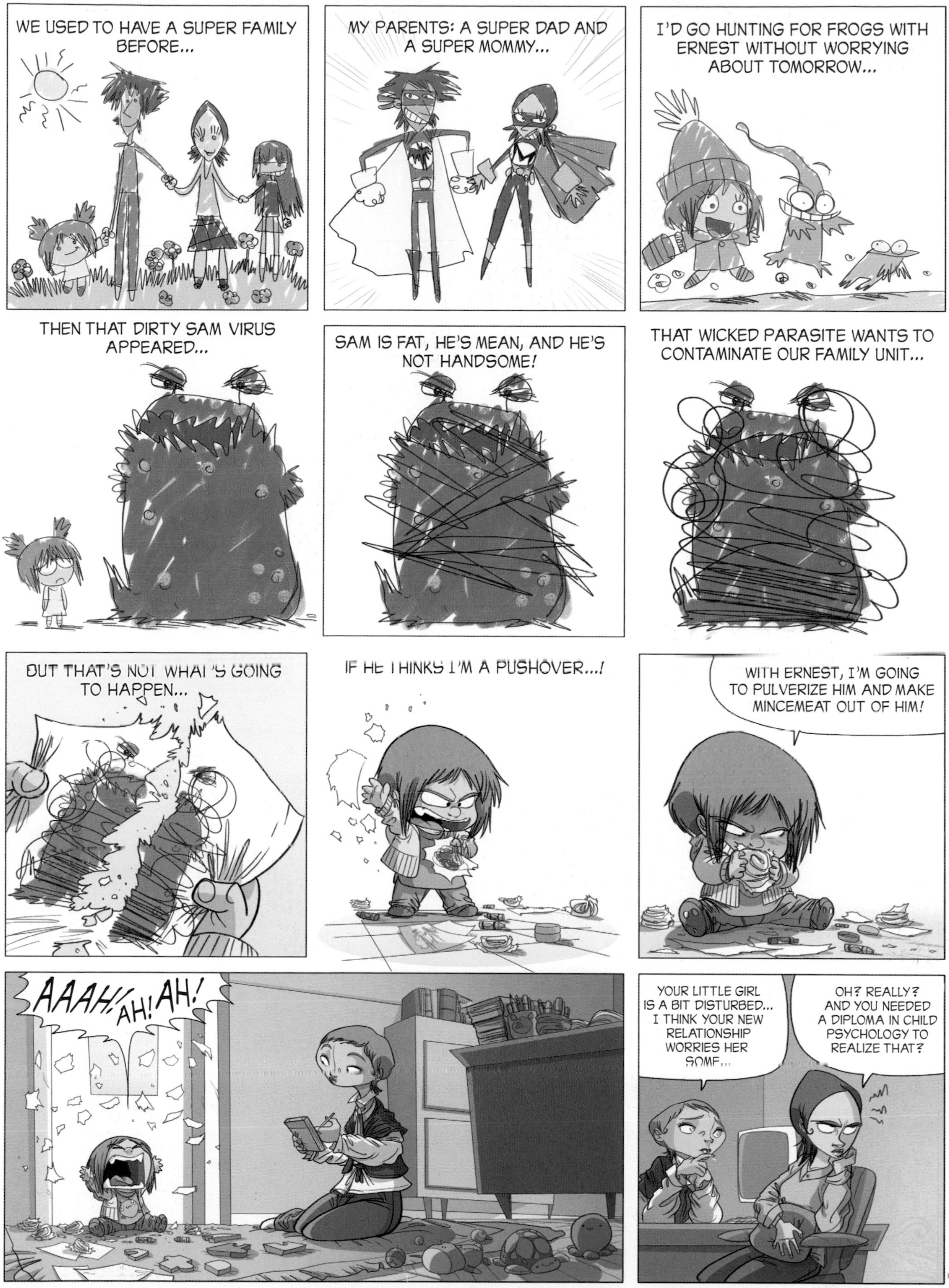

WE USED TO HAVE A SUPER FAMILY BEFORE...
MY PARENTS: A SUPER DAD AND A SUPER MOMMY...
I'D GO HUNTING FOR FROGS WITH ERNEST WITHOUT WORRYING ABOUT TOMORROW...
THEN THAT DIRTY SAM VIRUS APPEARED...
SAM IS FAT, HE'S MEAN, AND HE'S NOT HANDSOME!
THAT WICKED PARASITE WANTS TO CONTAMINATE OUR FAMILY UNIT...
BUT THAT'S NOT WHAT'S GOING TO HAPPEN...
IF HE THINKS I'M A PUSHOVER...!
WITH ERNEST, I'M GOING TO PULVERIZE HIM AND MAKE MINCEMEAT OUT OF HIM!
AAAH! AH! AH!
YOUR LITTLE GIRL IS A BIT DISTURBED... I THINK YOUR NEW RELATIONSHIP WORRIES HER SOME...
OH? REALLY? AND YOU NEEDED A DIPLOMA IN CHILD PSYCHOLOGY TO REALIZE THAT?

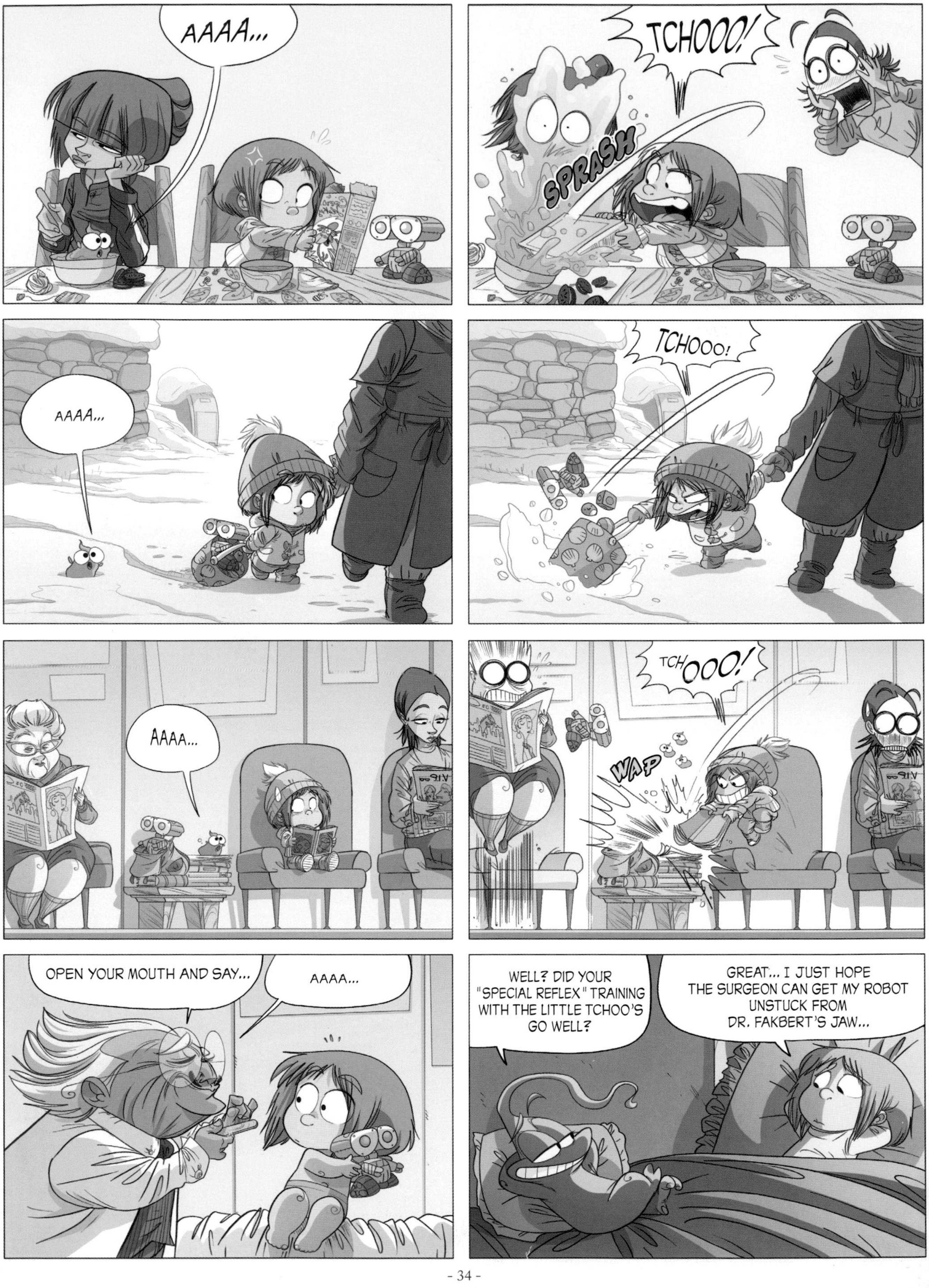
AAAA...
TCHOOO!
SPRASH
AAAA...
TCHOOO!
AAAA...
TCHOOO!
WAP
OPEN YOUR MOUTH AND SAY...
AAAA...
WELL? DID YOUR "SPECIAL REFLEX" TRAINING WITH THE LITTLE TCHOO'S GO WELL?
GREAT... I JUST HOPE THE SURGEON CAN GET MY ROBOT UNSTUCK FROM DR. FAKBERT'S JAW...

HAVE YOU EVER WONDERED WHERE THOSE HORRIBLE RED BUMPS THAT ITCH HORRIBLY MIGHT COME FROM?

UH... NO.

THEY'RE THE SYMPTOMS OF A MICROBIAL INFECTION...

SCRATCH

SCRATCH

SCRATCH

ARGH! I CAN'T STAND IT!

WE MICROBES ARE EXPERTS IN THE MATTER... FOR US, IT'S A NATIONAL SPORT...

I'M THE BEST!

THANKS TO OUR "DNA" CATAPULT MEMBRANE, WE'RE ABLE TO CONTAMINATE FROM A DISTANCE...

BLUB BLUB

ONE... TWO...

...THREE!

PTOU

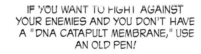

WE NEVER MISS OUR TARGET!

EEE! STOP, I SURRENDER!

...NEVER!

100.04°... SHE HAS A SLIGHT FEVER...

BUHHHH...

IF YOU WANT TO FIGHT AGAINST YOUR ENEMIES AND YOU DON'T HAVE A "DNA CATAPULT MEMBRANE," USE AN OLD PEN!

SOME PAPER MÂCHÉ DIPPED IN PINK INK WILL REALLY DO THE TRICK...

THAT WAY, YOU CAN DEFEAT YOUR TOUGHEST ADVERSARIES WITH NO PROBLEM!

REBECCAAA! WHAT **HAVE** YOU...

⇒PTOOO!⇐

OUCH!

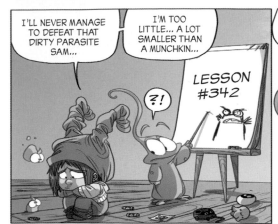

I'LL NEVER MANAGE TO DEFEAT THAT DIRTY PARASITE SAM...

I'M TOO LITTLE... A LOT SMALLER THAN A MUNCHKIN...

?!

LESSON #342

OH, YES? AND WHAT DO YOU MAKE OF DAVID AND GOLIATH? YOU KNOW, BEING LITTLE IS HARDLY AN INCONVENIENCE!

ON THE OTHER HAND, AN ADVERSARY THREE TIMES BIGGER THAN YOU...

BLUB

BLUB

...HAS THREE TIMES MORE PLACES TO BE HIT!

SO, HE'S THREE TIMES MORE VULNERABLE!

WOW!

THE SMALLER YOU ARE...

WHAT'S MORE, YOU'RE OUT OF REACH...

...BUT NO LESS DANGEROUS FOR ALL THAT! ⸰GNAP!⸰

OUCH! MY FOOT!

WITH MICROBES, BEING BIG IS A WEAKNESS AND BEING SMALL AN ADVANTAGE!

REMEMBER THAT WELL, LITTLE M--⸰

POW

AND WHAT DO YOU SAY ABOUT THAT, HMMM?

I SAY YOU'RE NOT LISTENING...

"LITTLE" "MINISCULE"

"MICROSCOPIC"

"BUT NO LESS DANGEROUS FOR ALL THAT"! TICKLE TICKLE!

HEE HEE! STOP, ERNEST! I UNDERSTOOD THE LESSON! HEE HEE!

SCRATCH

SCRATCH

INSECTS, MICROBES, MITES...

"TINY, BUT STRONG"!

NO MORE SOUP EVER. I'VE DECIDED TO STOP MY GROWTH. IT'S A QUESTION OF SURVIVAL!

OKAY, LET'S KEEP CALM.

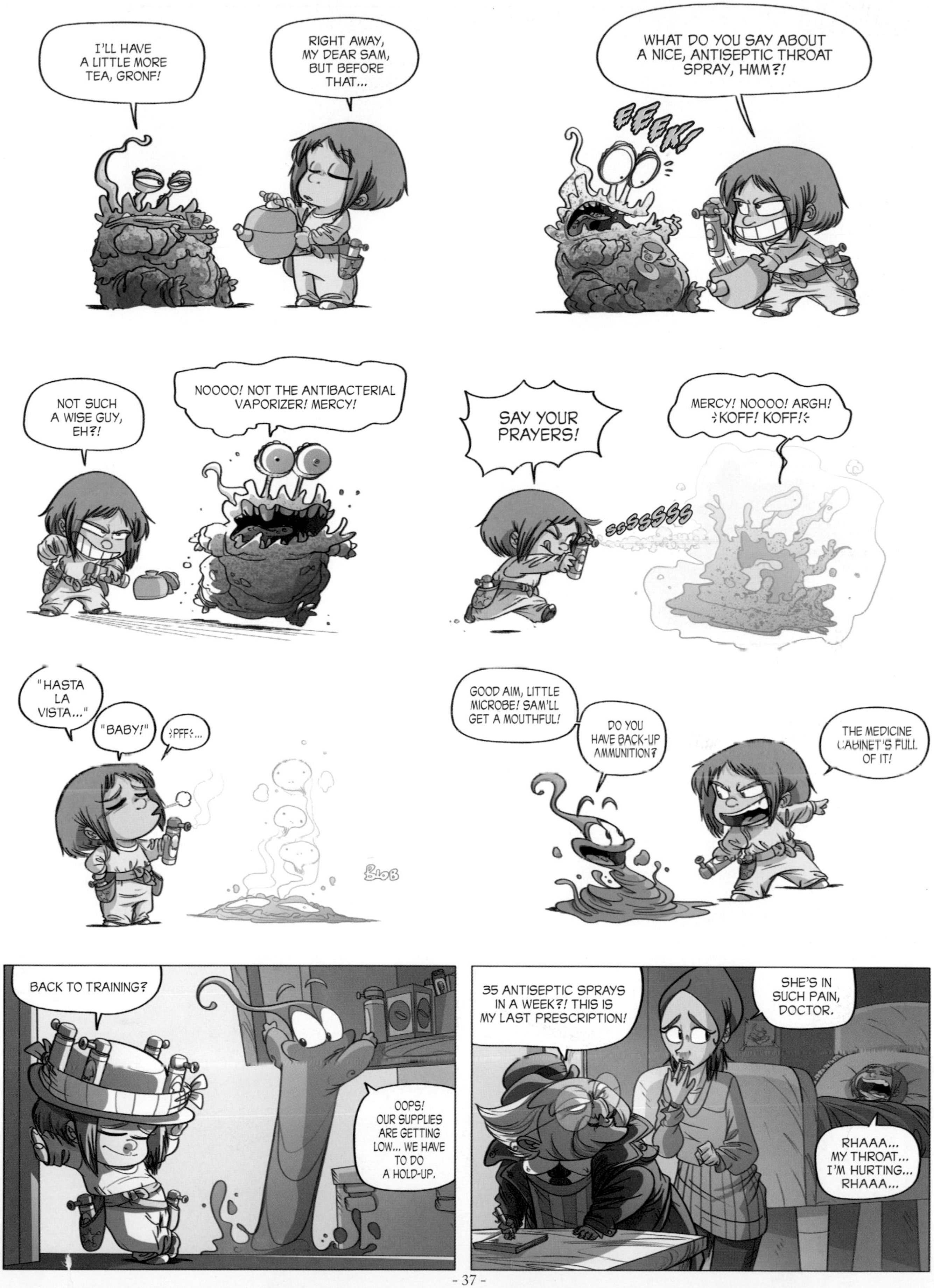

I'LL HAVE A LITTLE MORE TEA, GRONF!
RIGHT AWAY, MY DEAR SAM, BUT BEFORE THAT...
WHAT DO YOU SAY ABOUT A NICE, ANTISEPTIC THROAT SPRAY, HMM?!
EEEK!
NOT SUCH A WISE GUY, EH?!
NOOOO! NOT THE ANTIBACTERIAL VAPORIZER! MERCY!
SAY YOUR PRAYERS!
SSSSSSS
MERCY! NOOOO! ARGH! KOFF! KOFF!
"HASTA LA VISTA..."
"BABY!"
PFF...
GOOD AIM, LITTLE MICROBE! SAM'LL GET A MOUTHFUL!
DO YOU HAVE BACK-UP AMMUNITION?
THE MEDICINE CABINET'S FULL OF IT!
BACK TO TRAINING?
OOPS! OUR SUPPLIES ARE GETTING LOW... WE HAVE TO DO A HOLD-UP.
35 ANTISEPTIC SPRAYS IN A WEEK?! THIS IS MY LAST PRESCRIPTION!
SHE'S IN SUCH PAIN, DOCTOR.
RHAAA... MY THROAT... I'M HURTING... RHAAA...

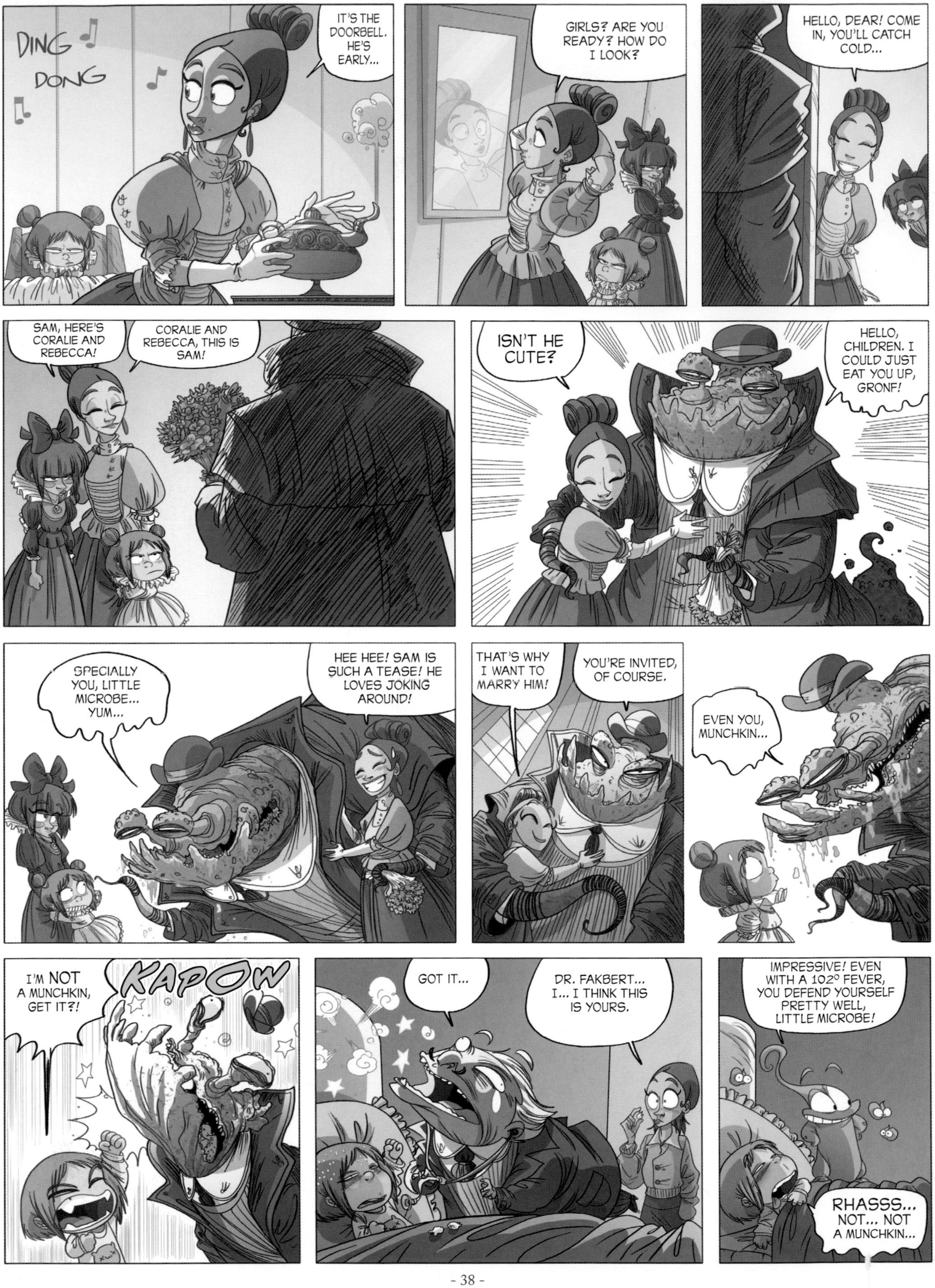
DING DONG
IT'S THE DOORBELL. HE'S EARLY...
GIRLS? ARE YOU READY? HOW DO I LOOK?
HELLO, DEAR! COME IN, YOU'LL CATCH COLD...
SAM, HERE'S CORALIE AND REBECCA!
CORALIE AND REBECCA, THIS IS SAM!
ISN'T HE CUTE?
HELLO, CHILDREN. I COULD JUST EAT YOU UP, GRONF!
SPECIALLY YOU, LITTLE MICROBE... YUM...
HEE HEE! SAM IS SUCH A TEASE! HE LOVES JOKING AROUND!
THAT'S WHY I WANT TO MARRY HIM!
YOU'RE INVITED, OF COURSE.
EVEN YOU, MUNCHKIN...
I'M NOT A MUNCHKIN, GET IT?!
KAPOW
GOT IT...
DR. FAKBERT... I... I THINK THIS IS YOURS.
IMPRESSIVE! EVEN WITH A 102° FEVER, YOU DEFEND YOURSELF PRETTY WELL, LITTLE MICROBE!
RHASSS... NOT... NOT A MUNCHKIN...

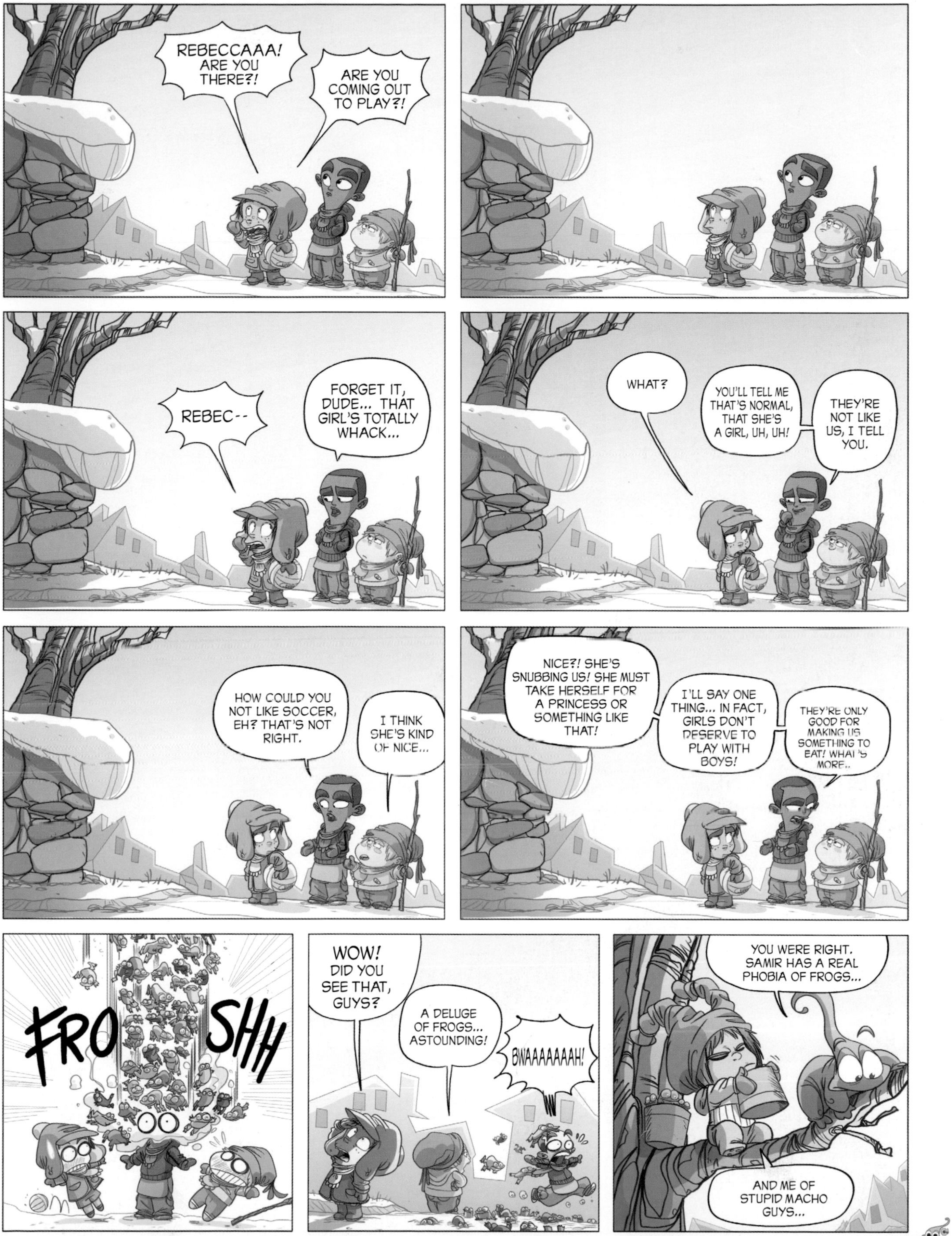
REBECCAAA! ARE YOU THERE?!
ARE YOU COMING OUT TO PLAY?!
REBEC--
FORGET IT, DUDE... THAT GIRL'S TOTALLY WHACK...
WHAT?
YOU'LL TELL ME THAT'S NORMAL, THAT SHE'S A GIRL, UH, UH!
THEY'RE NOT LIKE US, I TELL YOU.
HOW COULD YOU NOT LIKE SOCCER, EH? THAT'S NOT RIGHT.
I THINK SHE'S KIND OF NICE...
NICE?! SHE'S SNUBBING US! SHE MUST TAKE HERSELF FOR A PRINCESS OR SOMETHING LIKE THAT!
I'LL SAY ONE THING... IN FACT, GIRLS DON'T DESERVE TO PLAY WITH BOYS!
THEY'RE ONLY GOOD FOR MAKING US SOMETHING TO EAT! WHAT'S MORE..
FRO SHH
WOW! DID YOU SEE THAT, GUYS?
A DELUGE OF FROGS... ASTOUNDING!
BWAAAAAAAH!
YOU WERE RIGHT. SAMIR HAS A REAL PHOBIA OF FROGS...
AND ME OF STUPID MACHO GUYS...

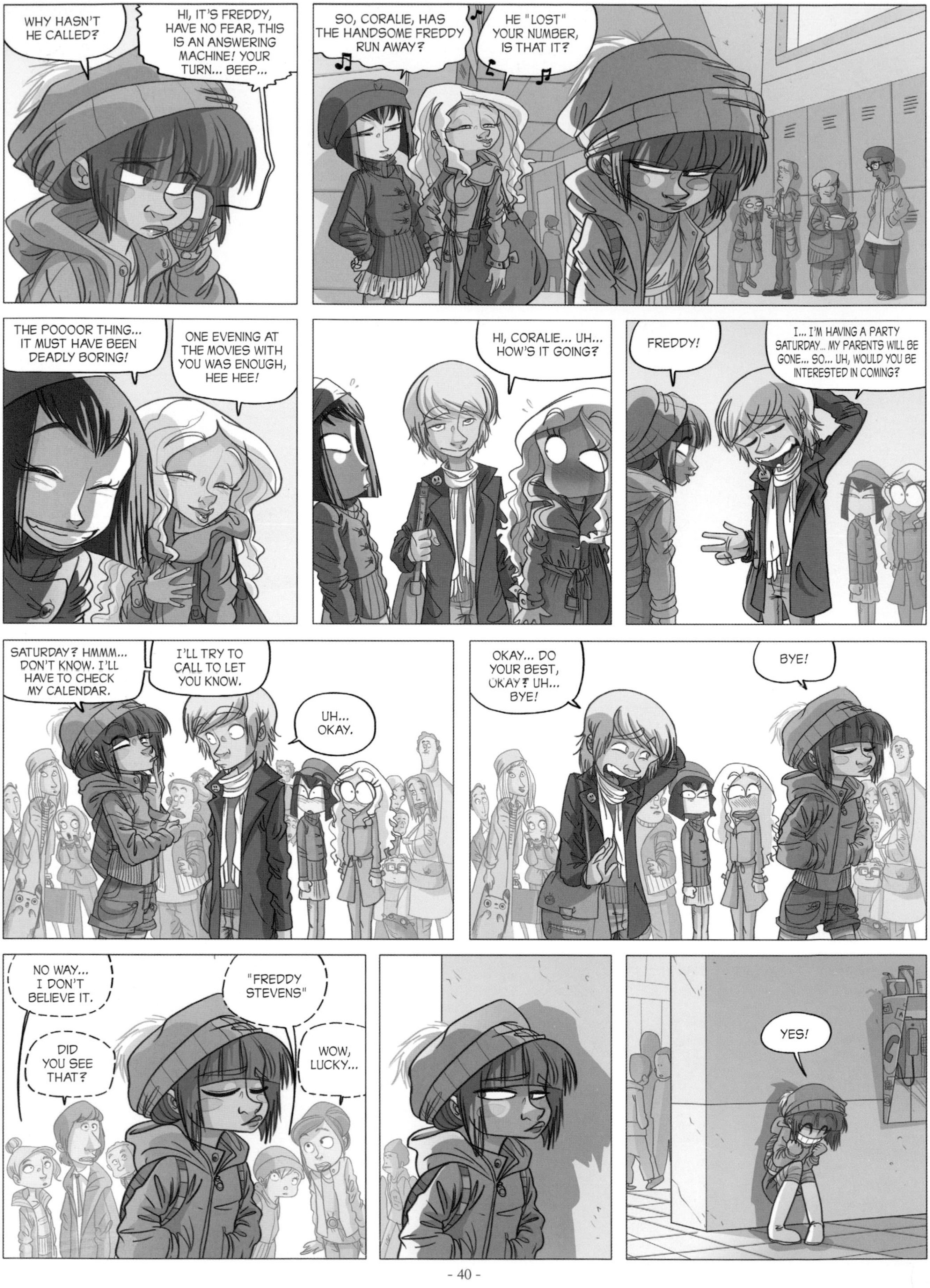
WHY HASN'T HE CALLED?
HI, IT'S FREDDY, HAVE NO FEAR, THIS IS AN ANSWERING MACHINE! YOUR TURN... BEEP...
SO, CORALIE, HAS THE HANDSOME FREDDY RUN AWAY?
HE "LOST" YOUR NUMBER, IS THAT IT?
THE POOOOR THING... IT MUST HAVE BEEN DEADLY BORING!
ONE EVENING AT THE MOVIES WITH YOU WAS ENOUGH, HEE HEE!
HI, CORALIE... UH... HOW'S IT GOING?
FREDDY!
I... I'M HAVING A PARTY SATURDAY... MY PARENTS WILL BE GONE... SO... UH, WOULD YOU BE INTERESTED IN COMING?
SATURDAY? HMMM... DON'T KNOW. I'LL HAVE TO CHECK MY CALENDAR.
I'LL TRY TO CALL TO LET YOU KNOW.
UH... OKAY.
OKAY... DO YOUR BEST, OKAY? UH... BYE!
BYE!
NO WAY... I DON'T BELIEVE IT.
"FREDDY STEVENS"
DID YOU SEE THAT?
WOW, LUCKY...
YES!

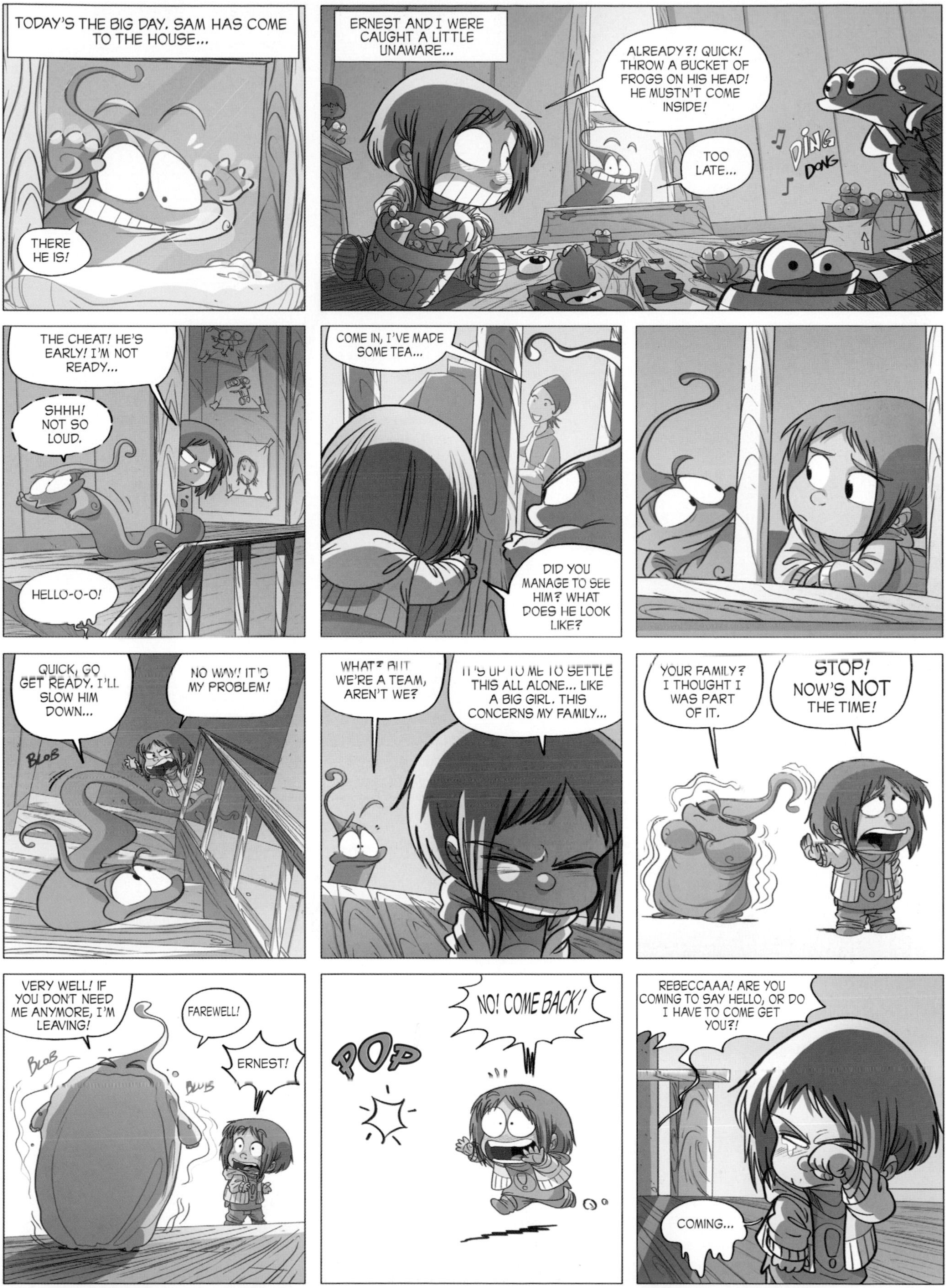
TODAY'S THE BIG DAY. SAM HAS COME TO THE HOUSE...
THERE HE IS!
ERNEST AND I WERE CAUGHT A LITTLE UNAWARE...
ALREADY?! QUICK! THROW A BUCKET OF FROGS ON HIS HEAD! HE MUSTN'T COME INSIDE!
TOO LATE...
DING
DONG
THE CHEAT! HE'S EARLY! I'M NOT READY...
SHHH! NOT SO LOUD.
HELLO-O-O!
COME IN, I'VE MADE SOME TEA...
DID YOU MANAGE TO SEE HIM? WHAT DOES HE LOOK LIKE?
QUICK, GO GET READY. I'LL SLOW HIM DOWN...
NO WAY! IT'S MY PROBLEM!
BLOB
WHAT? BUT WE'RE A TEAM, AREN'T WE?
IT'S UP TO ME TO SETTLE THIS ALL ALONE... LIKE A BIG GIRL. THIS CONCERNS MY FAMILY...
YOUR FAMILY? I THOUGHT I WAS PART OF IT.
STOP! NOW'S NOT THE TIME!
VERY WELL! IF YOU DON'T NEED ME ANYMORE, I'M LEAVING!
FAREWELL!
ERNEST!
BLOB
BLUB
NO! COME BACK!
POP
REBECCAAA! ARE YOU COMING TO SAY HELLO, OR DO I HAVE TO COME GET YOU?!
COMING...

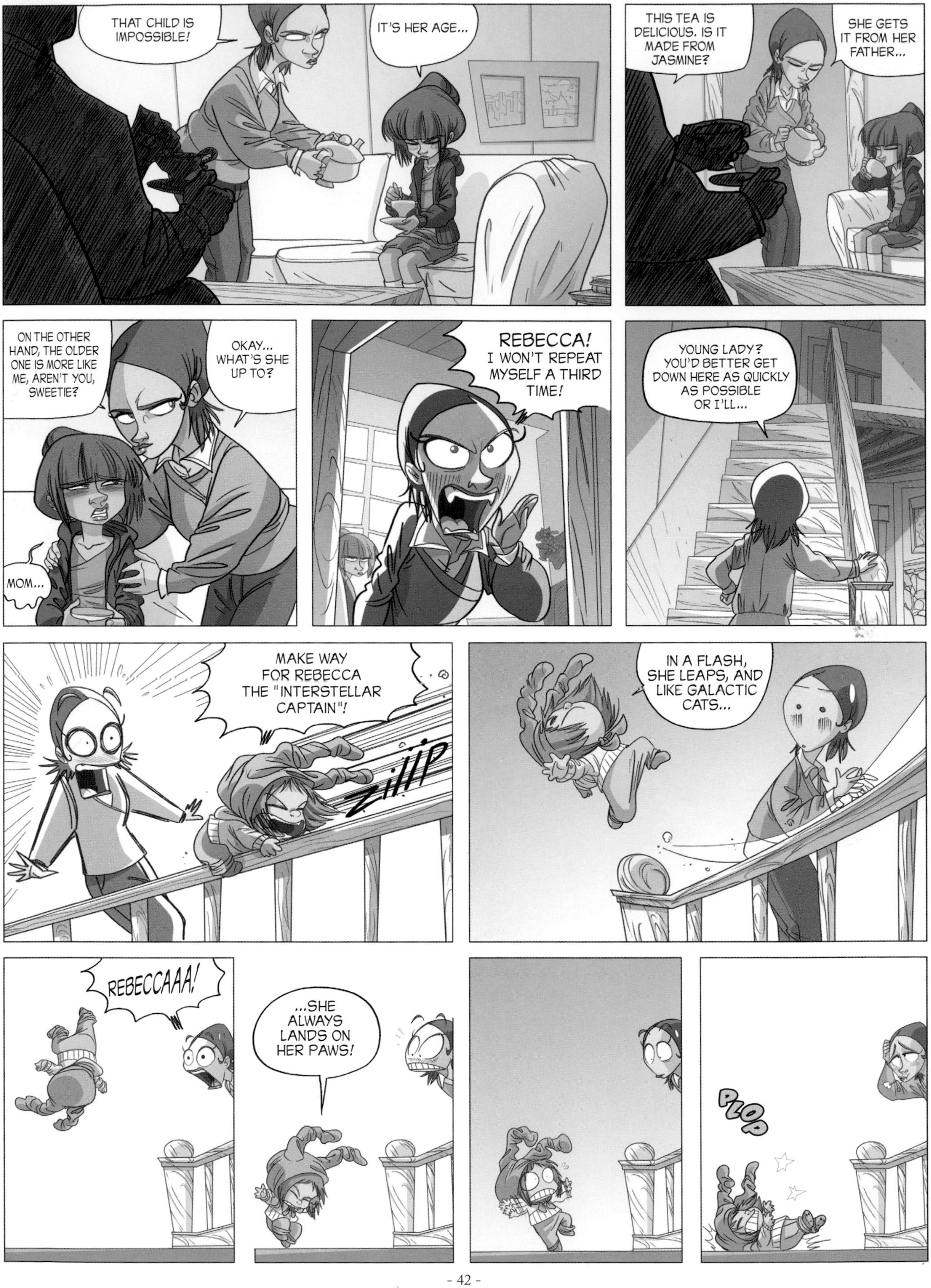
THAT CHILD IS IMPOSSIBLE!
IT'S HER AGE...
THIS TEA IS DELICIOUS. IS IT MADE FROM JASMINE?
SHE GETS IT FROM HER FATHER...
ON THE OTHER HAND, THE OLDER ONE IS MORE LIKE ME, AREN'T YOU, SWEETIE?
OKAY... WHAT'S SHE UP TO?
MOM...
REBECCA! I WON'T REPEAT MYSELF A THIRD TIME!
YOUNG LADY? YOU'D BETTER GET DOWN HERE AS QUICKLY AS POSSIBLE OR I'LL...
MAKE WAY FOR REBECCA THE "INTERSTELLAR CAPTAIN"!
ZIIIP
IN A FLASH, SHE LEAPS, AND LIKE GALACTIC CATS...
REBECCAAA!
...SHE ALWAYS LANDS ON HER PAWS!
PLOP

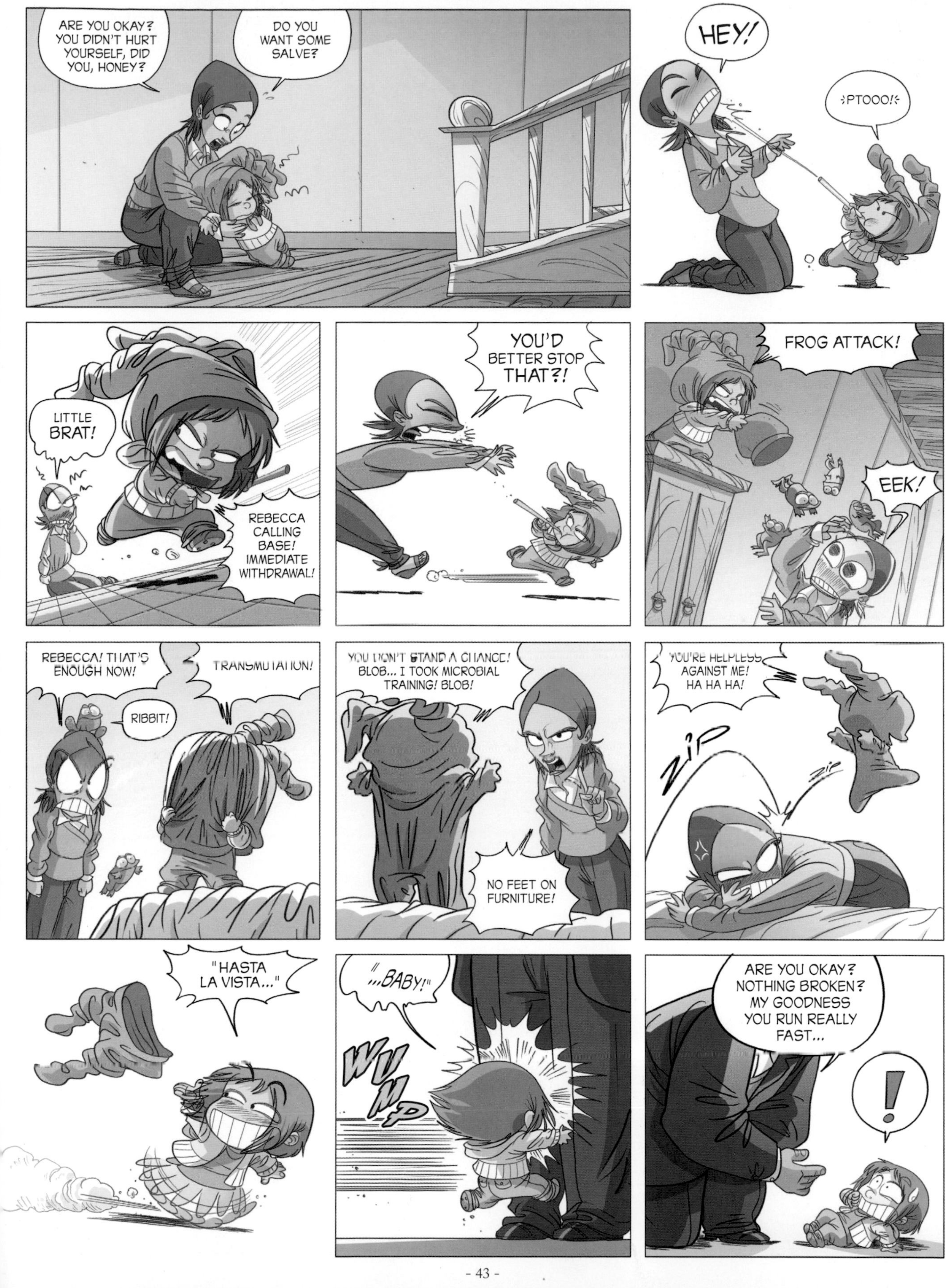

ARE YOU OKAY? YOU DIDN'T HURT YOURSELF, DID YOU, HONEY?
DO YOU WANT SOME SALVE?
HEY!
PTOOO!
LITTLE BRAT!
REBECCA CALLING BASE! IMMEDIATE WITHDRAWAL!
YOU'D BETTER STOP THAT?!
FROG ATTACK!
EEK!
REBECCA! THAT'S ENOUGH NOW!
TRANSMUTATION!
RIBBIT!
YOU DON'T STAND A CHANCE! BLOB... I TOOK MICROBIAL TRAINING! BLOB!
NO FEET ON FURNITURE!
YOU'RE HELPLESS AGAINST ME! HA HA HA!
ZIP
ZIP
"HASTA LA VISTA..."
"...BABY!"
WUMP
ARE YOU OKAY? NOTHING BROKEN? MY GOODNESS YOU RUN REALLY FAST...
!

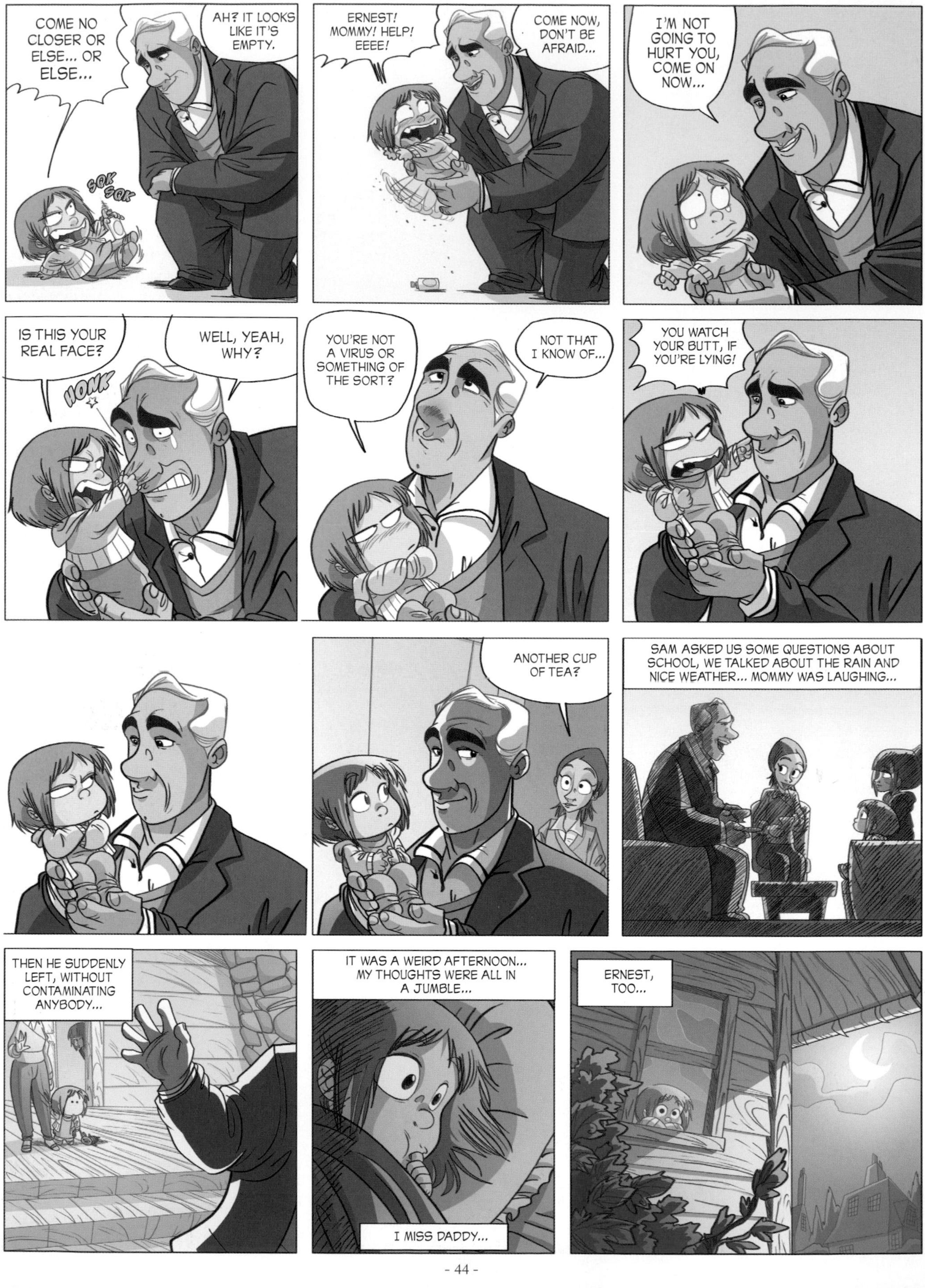
COME NO CLOSER OR ELSE... OR ELSE...
AH? IT LOOKS LIKE IT'S EMPTY.
SQK SQK
ERNEST! MOMMY! HELP! EEEE!
COME NOW, DON'T BE AFRAID...
I'M NOT GOING TO HURT YOU, COME ON NOW...
IS THIS YOUR REAL FACE?
HONK
WELL, YEAH, WHY?
YOU'RE NOT A VIRUS OR SOMETHING OF THE SORT?
NOT THAT I KNOW OF...
YOU WATCH YOUR BUTT, IF YOU'RE LYING!
ANOTHER CUP OF TEA?
SAM ASKED US SOME QUESTIONS ABOUT SCHOOL, WE TALKED ABOUT THE RAIN AND NICE WEATHER... MOMMY WAS LAUGHING...
THEN HE SUDDENLY LEFT, WITHOUT CONTAMINATING ANYBODY...
IT WAS A WEIRD AFTERNOON... MY THOUGHTS WERE ALL IN A JUMBLE...
I MISS DADDY...
ERNEST, TOO...

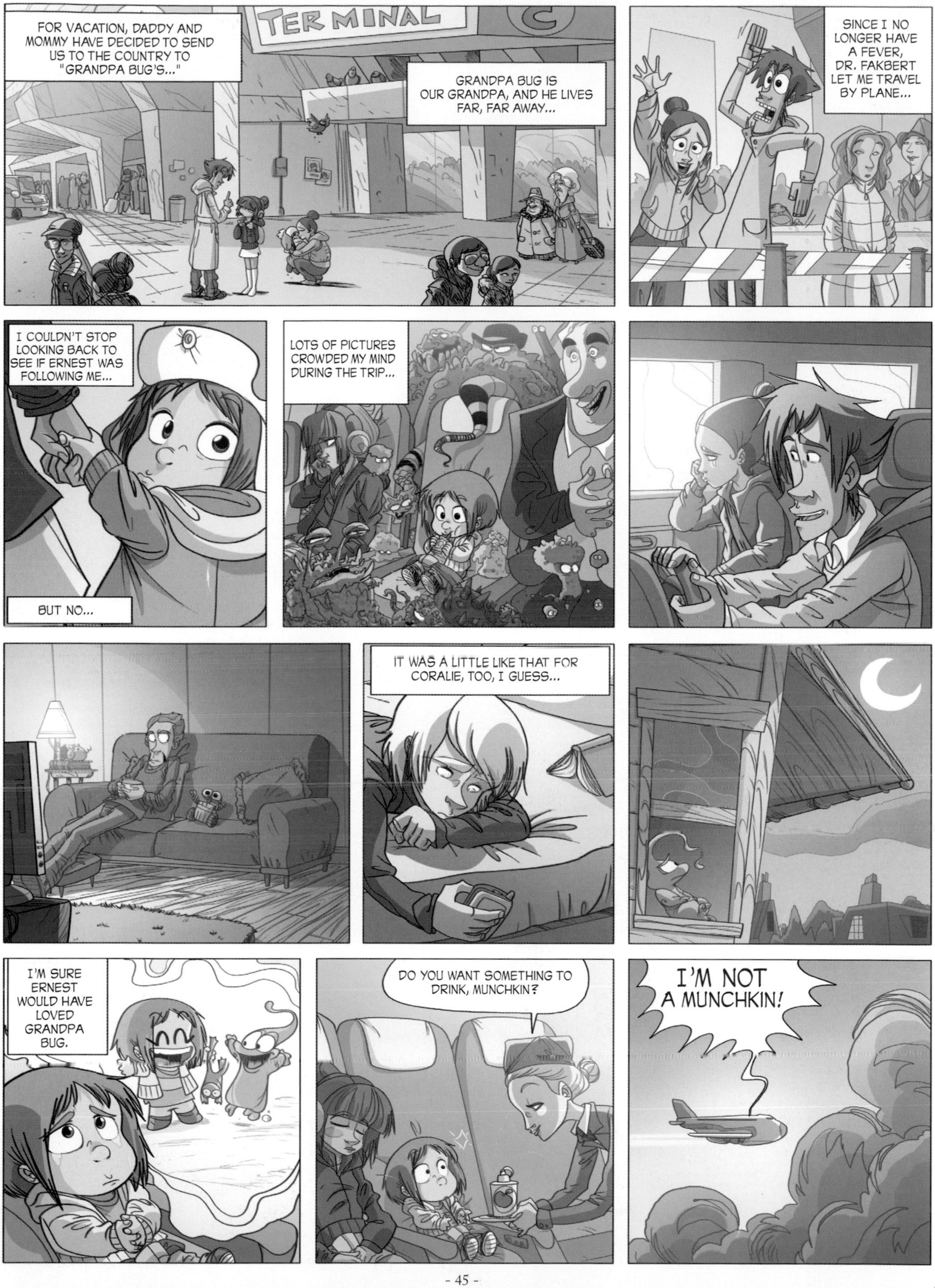
TERMINAL C
FOR VACATION, DADDY AND MOMMY HAVE DECIDED TO SEND US TO THE COUNTRY TO "GRANDPA BUG'S..."
GRANDPA BUG IS OUR GRANDPA, AND HE LIVES FAR, FAR AWAY...
SINCE I NO LONGER HAVE A FEVER, DR. FAKBERT LET ME TRAVEL BY PLANE...
I COULDN'T STOP LOOKING BACK TO SEE IF ERNEST WAS FOLLOWING ME...
BUT NO...
LOTS OF PICTURES CROWDED MY MIND DURING THE TRIP...
IT WAS A LITTLE LIKE THAT FOR CORALIE, TOO, I GUESS...
I'M SURE ERNEST WOULD HAVE LOVED GRANDPA BUG.
DO YOU WANT SOMETHING TO DRINK, MUNCHKIN?
I'M NOT A MUNCHKIN!

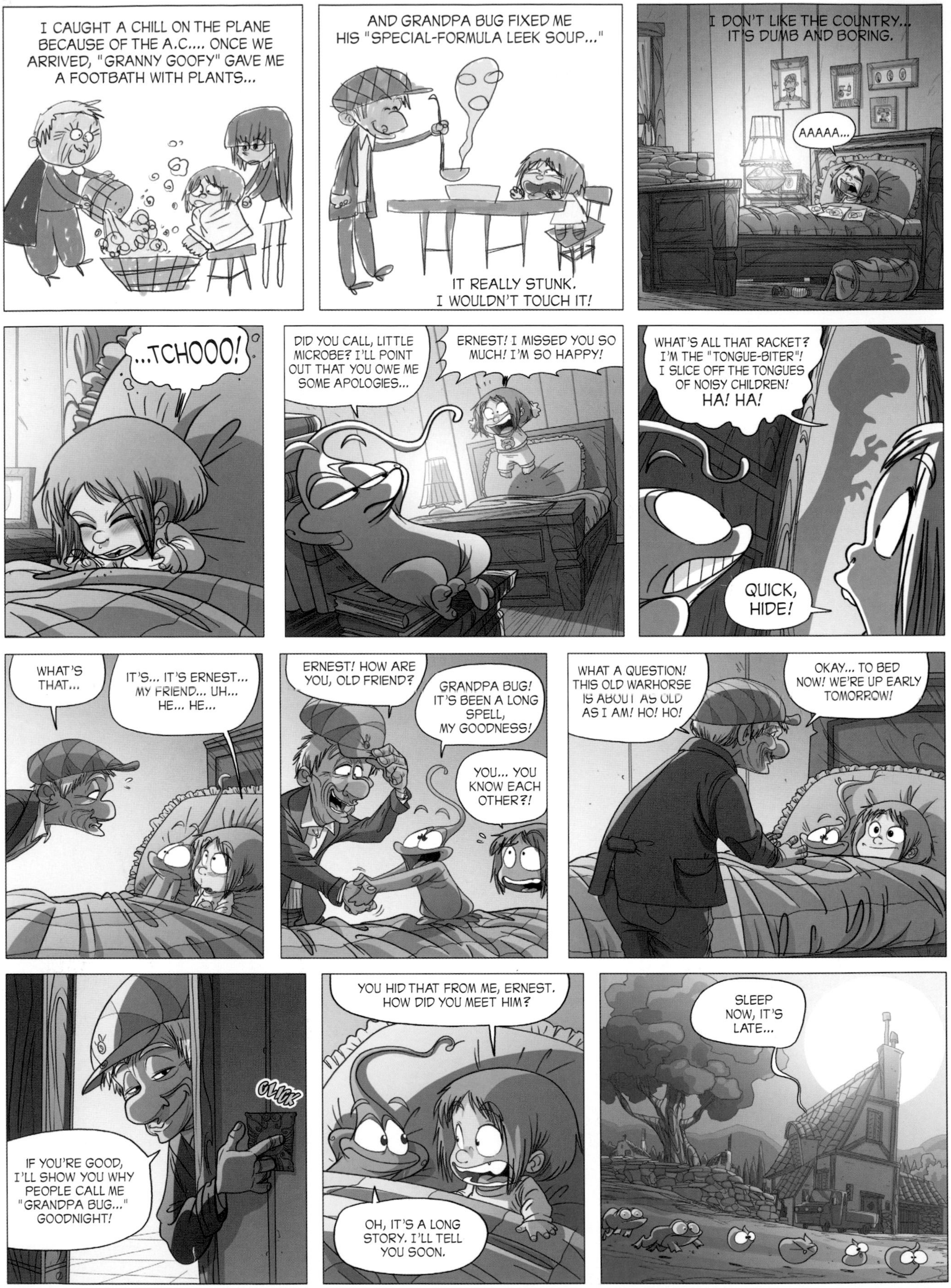
I CAUGHT A CHILL ON THE PLANE BECAUSE OF THE A.C.... ONCE WE ARRIVED, "GRANNY GOOFY" GAVE ME A FOOTBATH WITH PLANTS...
AND GRANDPA BUG FIXED ME HIS "SPECIAL-FORMULA LEEK SOUP..."
IT REALLY STUNK. I WOULDN'T TOUCH IT!
I DON'T LIKE THE COUNTRY... IT'S DUMB AND BORING.
AAAAA...
...TCHOOO!
DID YOU CALL, LITTLE MICROBE? I'LL POINT OUT THAT YOU OWE ME SOME APOLOGIES...
ERNEST! I MISSED YOU SO MUCH! I'M SO HAPPY!
WHAT'S ALL THAT RACKET? I'M THE "TONGUE-BITER"! I SLICE OFF THE TONGUES OF NOISY CHILDREN! HA! HA!
QUICK, HIDE!
WHAT'S THAT...
IT'S... IT'S ERNEST... MY FRIEND... UH... HE... HE...
ERNEST! HOW ARE YOU, OLD FRIEND?
GRANDPA BUG! IT'S BEEN A LONG SPELL, MY GOODNESS!
YOU... YOU KNOW EACH OTHER?!
WHAT A QUESTION! THIS OLD WARHORSE IS ABOUT AS OLD AS I AM! HO! HO!
OKAY... TO BED NOW! WE'RE UP EARLY TOMORROW!
CLICK
IF YOU'RE GOOD, I'LL SHOW YOU WHY PEOPLE CALL ME "GRANDPA BUG..." GOODNIGHT!
YOU HID THAT FROM ME, ERNEST. HOW DID YOU MEET HIM?
OH, IT'S A LONG STORY. I'LL TELL YOU SOON.
SLEEP NOW, IT'S LATE...

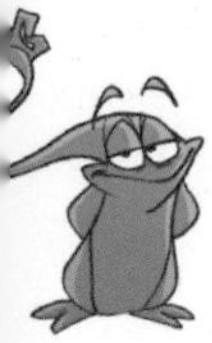

WATCH OUT FOR PAPERCUTZ™

Welcome to the second, slightly sentimental ERNEST & REBECCA graphic novel by Guillaume Bianco and Antonello Dalena. I'm Jim Salicrup, Editor-in-Chief of Papercutz, the company dedicated to publishing great graphic novels for all ages. And if ever there's a graphic novel series that's perfect for all ages, it's ERNEST & REBECCA!

Unlike many comics series that feature characters locked into a never-ending status quo, ERNEST & REBECCA is all about change. Starting with the first volume, "By Best Friend is a Germ," it's clear that we're meeting Rebecca's family at a crucial turning point—her parents are breaking up. This is an all-too common occurrence in modern family life, and it's always hard on the children.

But Rebecca's one tough little girl, and she isn't going to sit back and watch her family split apart. Working with Ernest she tries everything she can to get her mom and dad back together. But, as you know if you've read this volume, "Sam the Repulsive," it may already be too late. So, within the span of just two ERNEST & REBECCA graphic novels, Rebecca's life has changed drastically. Just like what happens to all of us in real life—change happens. Sometimes for the better, sometimes not. All we can do is keep going. In fact, there's a little poem I love that expresses that very idea, and I'd like to share it with you now:

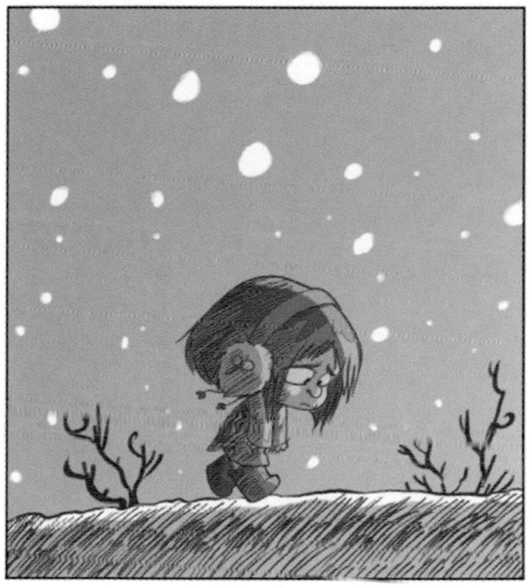

KEEP A-GOIN'
by Frank L. Stanton (1857-1927)

If you strike a thorn or rose,
Keep a-goin'!
If it hails or if it snows,
Keep a-goin'!
'Taint no use to sit an' whine
When the fish ain't on your line;
Bait your hook an' keep a-tryin'--
Keep a-goin'!

When the weather kills your crop,
Keep a-goin'!
Though 'tis work to reach the top,
Keep a-goin'!
S'pose you're out o' ev'ry dime,
Gittin' broke ain't any crime;
Tell the world you're feelin' prime--
Keep a-goin'!

When it looks like all is up,
Keep a-goin'!
Drain the sweetness from the cup,
Keep a-goin'!
See the wild birds on the wing,
Hear the bells that sweetly ring,
When you feel like singin', sing--
Keep a-goin'!

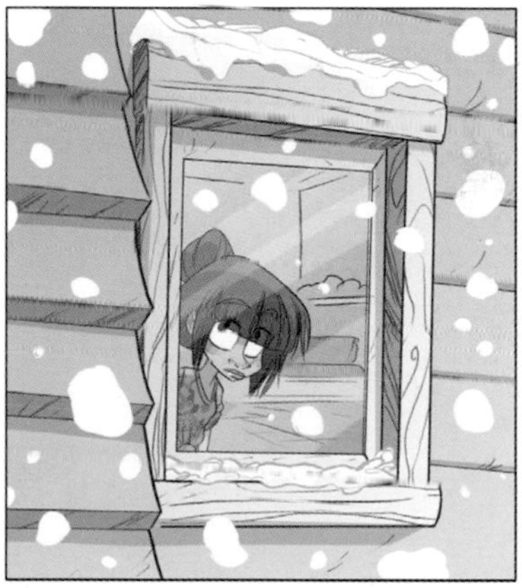

And all I can add to that uplifting poem, is a few words once sung by the great philosopher Daffy Duck, "You never know where you're goin' 'till you get there!" And that's also what makes life so exciting. Whether it's in our lives or in Rebecca's. For example, everything changes again, as the last few pages indicated, when Rebecca, Ernest, and Coralie are sent to visit their grandfather in ERNEST & REBECCA #3 "Grandpa Bug," coming soon to booksellers and comicbook stores everywhere.

In the meantime, you may want to check out such other Papercutz graphic novels as DANCE CLASS, DISNEY FAIRIES, GARFIELD & Co, GERONIMO STILTON, MONSTER, LEGO ® NINJAGO, THE SMURFS, SYBIL THE BACKPACK FAIRY, and more. For more information on Papercutz graphic novels go to www.papercutz.com. Surely, you'll find something to amuse you as you await the publication of ERNEST & REBECCA #3 "Grandpa Bug"!

Oh, one last thing. As we all know, being sick is no fun. We know that you're smart enough not to imitate any of the crazy things Rebecca does to make herself sick. She does it so that she can continue to see Ernest, but all we have to do to see Ernest is pick up an ERNEST & REBBECCA graphic novel. So, until we meet again, don't be making any snow angels in your underwear!

Thanks,

Jim

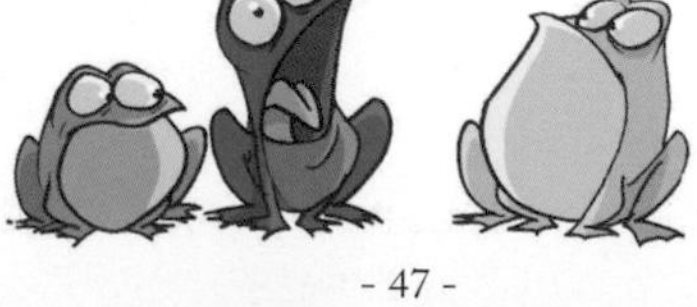

SEE ERNEST AND REBECCA
AGAIN VERY SOON
IN VOLUME 3, TITLED:
"GRANDPA BUG."

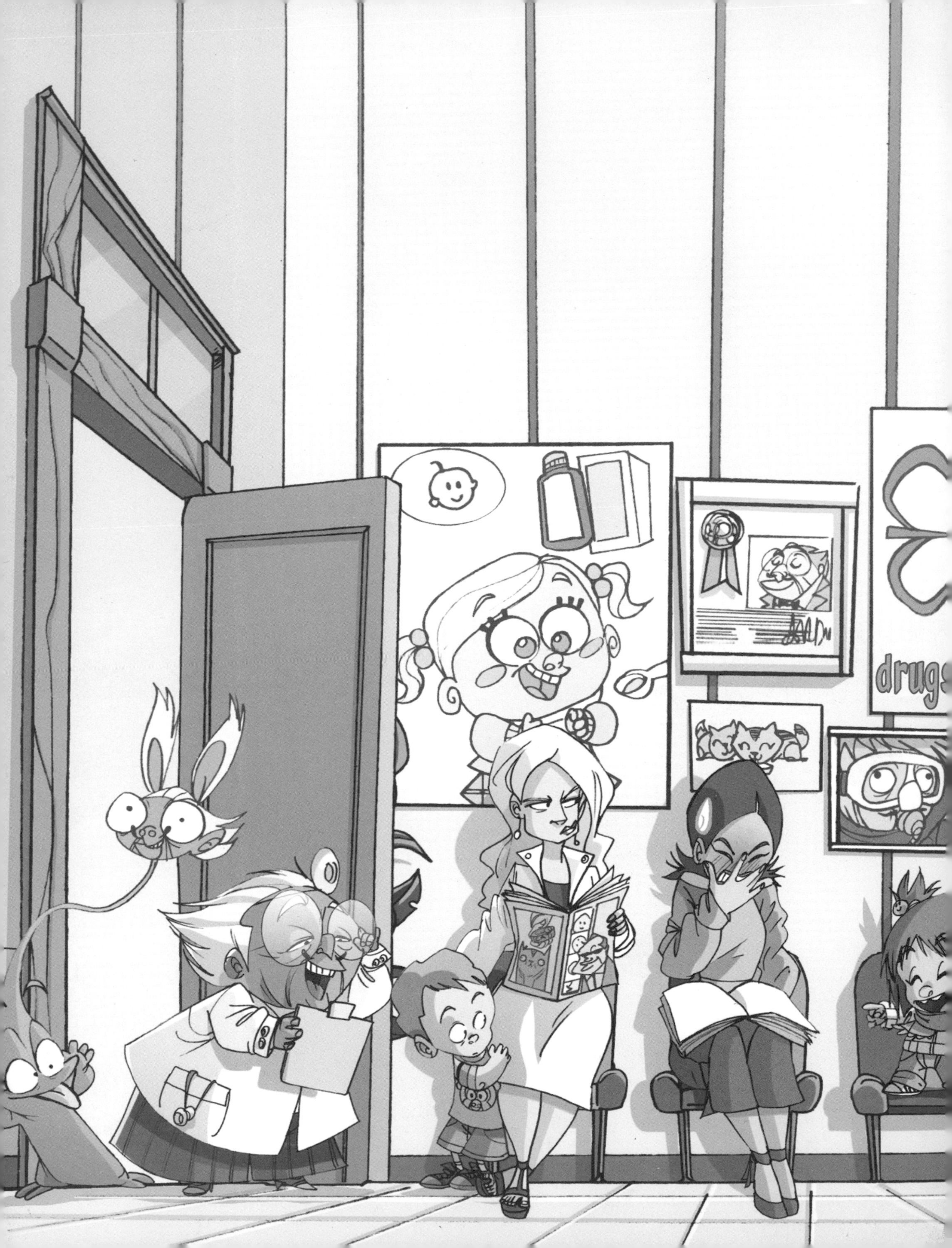
drugs